I0771895

rockettreehouse.com

Cover and interior design by Andy Hastings.
Edited by Kristen Stieffel and Scott Pearson.
Library of Congress Control Number: 2024921447
ISBN 979-8-9917443-2-4 (Paperback)
ISBN 979-8-9917443-0-0 (Hardcover)
ISBN 979-8-9917443-1-7 (eBook)
ISBN 979-8-9917443-3-1 (Audiobook)

For Caleb, Candace and Nathan

—my favorite space rangers.

Traversing the barren wastelands of space,

in the darkest corners of the solar system

which provide the slightest hint of comfort for only those

who choose to live outside the law,

a single representative of justice would dare to stand in the gap,

in the face of imminent danger and often insurmountable odds

as protector of the innocent.

The heroic deeds of the elite men and women

of the modern Space Ranger Corps are the stuff of legend.

A tradition began by their ancient counterparts—the Texas Rangers

of the Wild West—six-and-a-half centuries earlier.

ROBOT OF DEATH

Space Ranger Captain Jethro Rogers exhaled deeply and saw his own breath in the cold night air. The cloud of vapor caught a hightlight past the corner from which he was hiding. He grimaced and flattened tighter against the wall. Was it enough to give his position away? Did they already know he was there?

For a moment he waited and listened, his right hand slowly clenching and opening next to his holstered laser pistol. All seemed clear. He moved stealthily to the next shadowy crevice between the stacked shipping containers.

The late evening was quiet, as it usually was on the moon-based space port. Eerie, spider-like shadows fingered their way across the loading docks. Earth was half illuminated, suspended low in the black sky above. It cast a fluorescent blueish glow that washed through arching iron girders supporting a cluster of giant dura-glass domes overhead.

"Frankie Malone!" Captain Rogers' voice broke the silence and echoed under the giant structure. "I have a warrant. You can't run forever."

Multiple laser blasts peppered the corner of the container next to Jett. Sparks showered and pieces of hot metal shrapnel from the storage unit fell at his feet.

"It always has to be the *hard* way," said Jett, holding his pistol up close, by his cheek. He had walked into an ambush, but they revealed themselves too soon.

He brushed a few glowing embers from his jacket sleeve, turned and slipped behind the next two rows of containers, working in a semicircle from his original position. Easing up to a support pillar, Jett peered around the edge. His hand rested on a control panel with two large buttons. Glancing up, he traced the conduit as it went up and over to a suspended motorized pulley system on the other side of the loading area. He pressed the top button. Electric motors hummed, and the pulley began to move.

The sudden motion drew the gangsters' fire again, revealing their pinpoint locations.

Jett stepped out and countered.

His shots were lightning quick, with lethal accuracy. The exchange was brief, a few flashes within the blink of an eye.

Weapon steady, ready for a possible second exchange, Jett waited for the smoke to clear, alert eyes scanning his surroundings.

Four bodies lay in the alley ahead of him. One lay half exposed from the shadow of a dark corner. Two had fallen about twenty feet from their perch high atop some stacked containers to the alleyway floor below. The last had slumped over the controls of a forked lifting machine, causing it to jerk wildly, tearing a gash in the wall large enough for a man to walk through. Each body had a single small trail of smoke slowly dissipating above dark scorches, like four candles that had been swiftly extinguished.

The ranger strained to listen. All was once again quiet, except for the sound of a single pair of shoes fleeing through the gash in the wall—Frankie Malone.

The ranger gave chase. Entering the warehouse through the opening, he barely caught a glimpse of Frankie before he disappeared behind some circuit panels at the end of the catwalk. He was running for his life and didn't dare look back.

Jett found himself standing on a metallic mesh gangway, many stories above the building's floor. It was the electric generator room for Zone 3 of the loading docks. Below looked like a small city of generators and turbines, topped with an army of electric insulators that rose up toward him like ceramic ice-cream cones.

The air crackled with sizzling and popping from enormous amounts of electricity dancing along twisting copper cables that curved upward like giant curly-swoop soda straws.

Standing on the tremoring surface, the ranger felt more than heard a low hum from the turbines below, as it vibrated up through his bones and into his ears. This was a good place for a desperate fleeing criminal to hide and a dangerous place for a ranger who had just lost sight of his fugitive.

The ranger needed a better view; he needed to get higher.

Mounted to the wall near where he entered was a turbo-lift platform that ascended to a smaller maintenance catwalk running along the ceiling above the whole power plant.

Arriving at the top, he could see everything. Frankie would expect pursuit from behind and not think to look up.

Cautiously, Jett stepped toward the center of the catwalk, quickly scanning the maze below, left then right. He kept his eyes peeled for any movement, a glimpse of an elbow, the barrel of a gun sticking from behind a corner, any small thing that was out of the ordinary. But this whole place was out of the ordinary, with many distractions from the noise and sizzling electricity. One wrong step could mean instant death.

The temperature in this room was noticeably warmer than the air just outside. The volume of electricity produced by the myriad of giant turbines was enough to make a man start perspiring almost immediately. If not for the switching of duty every two hours from one half of the turbines to the other, they would eventually overheat. The transition was virtually seamless, with the only noticeable effect being the momentary dimming of the lights overhead.

When this occurred, Jett glanced up reflexively to see what was happening. Unfortunately, so did Frankie.

Startled to see his pursuer above him, the criminal sent a desperately wild shot—missing the ranger completely, but striking the catwalk squarely, severing it in half and taking a few suspension cables with it.

The total weight of the severed catwalk was too much for the remaining cables to bear. Immediately, with increasing rapidity, they began to snap loose. *Snap. Snap snap snap.* Then the whole structure gave way, swinging downward like a giant hinge, still attached to the far wall. The catwalk dropped beneath his feet like a trap door, sending the ranger plummeting toward one of the sizzling electric turbines below.

There was no time to think. Jett saw a hanging cable about fifteen feet away. If he jumped with all his might, he just might be able to make it. It was his only chance—he went for it.

His left hand slipped, and the cable slid up his arm to his shoulder as he began to fall. He let go of his gun and slammed his right hand to his chest, trapping the cable against his body, fumbling to find it, then gripping tightly. He swung out in a large, swooping curve as he glimpsed a dizzy drop below and watched his pistol fall, smashing on the spinning turbines.

The ranger's momentum swung him around, then sent him straight toward Frankie, staring aghast, on the lower catwalk. The criminal was so stunned at the display of swashbuckling agility, he almost forgot about his opportunity to shoot until he saw the ranger careening toward him.

Once again, more reflexively than with purpose, Frankie wildly fired as many desperate blasts as he could; he only got off three. One went astray. The second went through the sleeve of the ranger, missing his arm, but leaving a stinging burn. The third and last shot completely severed the cable just above his hands.

But by this time, Jett was close enough to give a precisely timed and perfectly aimed forward thrust-kick, sending Frankie to his back and the laser gun sliding down the catwalk, yards behind him.

The ranger jumped to his feet, but Frankie had gotten up first. It was a race to the fallen gun. Jett took off across the catwalk in full sprint, tackling Frankie so hard they both almost went over the railing. With a quick, powerful thrust of his right palm to Frankie's throat, the ranger sent the criminal backward, stunned and fighting for air.

Very few are equal to a Space Ranger in hand-to-hand combat.

Jett rubbed his arm along the burned hole in his sleeve, picked up the gun, and kicked back to Frankie the fedora hat he had lost in the scuffle.

"I'll give you a second to catch your breath, Frankie, and then we'll be taking our little trip together. Your game of cat and mouse is finally over."

The gangster sat on the catwalk, his right palm flat to the floor, his left grasping his throat and rubbing. Strangely, a razor smile of satisfaction grew across his face, revealing crooked teeth.

What could he possibly be smiling about? Was it a bluff? Or did Frankie have more cohorts than Jett had previously counted on? Jett was sure there were only four others, and none of those was coming back to help. But what if he had miscalculated?

Jett heard a mechanical sound just behind him and the brief

whirring of electronic servos. He attempted to spin around but was caught abruptly. Two arms of iron wrapped around the ranger like a steel trap. His own arms were pinned to his side, and his chest creaked from the tremendous pressure. It was a robot, a heavy-duty worker robot from the loading docks outside.

The ranger's hands reflexively opened, and the gun fell to the catwalk by his feet. Frankie lunged for it. The only choice was to kick the gun over the side.

"You!" Frankie forced himself up, trembling from a combination of anger and shock. He positioned himself squarely in front of the ranger and threw a few jabs into his gut and one across his jaw. He would have thrown more, but Frankie sprained a finger with the last punch to the ranger's stout cheekbone.

Frankie rubbed his throat again and struggled to speak. "Now look here, you. You'll never get the best o' me, copper! Ya see? Betcha didn't expect this now, did ya? Ha!" The vocal strain was too much, and he coughed harshly. Frankie glanced at his watch and acted like he was late for something.

He stepped out of Jett's sight behind the robot. It sounded like he opened a rear panel and punched a few buttons. "Look here, robot. Suffocate 'im!" Then he came back around and grabbed the ranger by the chin. "Now let's see who's the cat and who's the mouse ... Mickey." Frankie broke into a wicked laugh that triggered another coughing fit. With some effort, he regained his composure and pointed at the ranger. "You gonna pay for whatcha did to my boys." He picked up his hat, straightened his trench coat, then spat. With a final harsh and grating wheeze, Frankie Malone hurriedly left the scene, holding his sore finger and rubbing his throat.

The bright-red robot was not programmed to think for itself, only to carry out its instructions perfectly to the letter. So began the squeezing of the ranger, to the point he could no longer breathe.

Jett glanced around, searching for anything that could ease his situation. Putting his feet up on the handrail in front of him, he pushed back against the robot with all the strength he had in his legs, trying to tip it backward so it would step to keep its equilibrium. It worked! Even though the robot was resisting, it was slowly moving in the direction the ranger wanted to steer it. He kept pushing, trying to guide it over to the service tool cabinet he had seen mounted to one of the circuit switcher boxes next to the catwalk. Time was getting short. If he didn't reach the toolbox before he passed out, it would all be over. Even if he did get there in time, he wondered if there would be anything in it that could possibly help.

Every muscle began to ache and scream for oxygen. His lungs burned like he had swallowed hot coals. His head, turning beet red, throbbed and pulsed with the blood that was frantically trying to deliver oxygen it did not have to his brain.

Every fiber of his body now craved a life-giving breath.

The robot, if it wanted, had the strength to simply crush the ranger and be done with its job in an instant. Fortunately for Jett, that was not the command it had been given, allowing the precious time he needed to get the robot over to the tool cabinet. As the mechanical menace clumsily banged into the locker, it jarred the door wide open and sent an assortment of tools cascading to the floor.

There, among the scattered tools, was a crowbar. Jett stretched with his foot as far as he could and was barely able to touch the crowbar with the tip of his boot. Coaxing the bar a few inches toward him at a time, after repeated pawings, he finally got it close enough to reach over with his other foot. With both feet together, he attempted to raise it. His grip was not good, and when he got the bar halfway up, it slipped, fell to the edge of the catwalk, and almost went over.

He was dizzy and felt as though he was about to faint. He only had one more attempt left in him. This last try would have to work. The bar was closer to him this time, so he was able to position his feet better and lift the bar successfully to his left hand.

Turning the bar around, he fished for a place where he could get some leverage under the robot's arm, a place where the tip of the crowbar wouldn't slip. A dent, a seam, anything.

He felt a bump on the outer shell of the robot's torso under its arm. Good enough. With his arms pinned, Jett pushed the best he could.

The bar slipped off the rounded edge, but not before it had raised the iron arm enough to allow him to gasp a breath. He performed this same maneuver several times until he was able to get his breath back somewhat, finding himself able to hold the arm up a little longer each time.

Even though he had found an opportunity to breathe a little, he was still desperate to get free from the robot. He didn't know how much longer he could withstand the pressure being applied to his chest.

Once again, he started fishing with the tip of the crowbar for a new place to dig into the robot's side, hoping to raise the arms up high enough to escape. After several unsuccessful attempts, fatigue set in. He relaxed, letting the bar slide down where it came to rest on a ledge of what felt like the robot's service panel. Jett pushed the metal bar, and it slid inside the small door; the robot, sensing the potential for a short circuit, threw him to the floor.

His lungs gulped air greedily. He was weak and his muscles burned, but he ran, fast as he could, determined not to let this mechanical crusher grab hold of him a second time.

Stumbling down the catwalk, he came to a T junction, stopped, and looked back. The robot advanced, eyes glowing orange and red, while two paneled doors on its chest swung open to reveal a deadly secret.

"What is this?" Jett muttered. His eyes went wide, and he swallowed hard. Twin, high-powered machine-gun blasters swung out and down, locking into place, and immediately commenced firing.

Jett dove to his right, taking cover behind a large circuit box hanging from the ceiling. *What was Frankie doing with this thing?* Worker robots were made to perform menial tasks, like lifting and cleaning and maintenance in dangerous places, but this looked like something created for war.

The walking destroyer fired a steady stream of laser blasts with the rapidity of a furious drum roll, making the rumble of the machines below pale in comparison. Debris fell and lodged in the spinning turbines. Sparks flew everywhere, and the lights overhead dimmed off and on. Giant blue currents of electricity arced up from the insulators below and grounded themselves onto the nearest, largest metal objects, like dancing artificial lightning bolts. The robot's single-mindedness to destroy the ranger, with total disregard for everything else around it, was wreaking havoc, and it was about to get worse.

If Jett didn't find a way out of there quickly, the building would be his tomb.

All the main exits were out of the question; he would be far too vulnerable, exposing himself to the robot's direct line of fire. He looked around and saw what he thought was his only option. It was a long shot, but his lungs and legs felt better, and as much as he despised relying on luck, he was going to need a lot of it. The ranger took off, the two breaker boxes fell, and the robot rounded the corner.

Jett made it to the east wall in time, dove behind the last

suspended breaker box, and eyed the maintenance service tunnel a little farther down. He would have to inch his way along a narrow ledge to get there. But first, he had to wait. If he went too soon, he would be dangerously exposed. As the robot got closer, he could gradually move back, keeping the breaker box between him and the robot as a shield. He only hoped it would stay up long enough to do the job; it was already pretty tattered and hanging at a precarious angle.

The robot kept advancing, about the pace of an average man's brisk walk. Its torso was able to swivel at the waist, allowing it to fire in a different direction from which it was walking.

With some distance still between the ranger and the tunnel, his shield gave way, exposing him to his executioner. The wall erupted next to Jett, showering him with large chunks of electrical tubing and pressurized pipe debris.

He leaped.

The tunnel was a round hole in the wall, about five feet in diameter. A horizontal shaft about fifteen feet deep, capped by a service hatch in the rear, led outside.

Laser blasts swept right, across the middle of the opening. The ranger hung from the bottom edge, fingers clasping the lower lip of the shaft.

The robot adjusted its aim and lowered its guns, preparing to sweep back to the left for a second pass.

Jett tried to switch his grip and put his back to the wall.

His hands were sweaty, and his left hand slipped as he made the adjustment. He dangled by his right hand and strained his fingers to hang on. He swung his legs to bring his left arm up and grasped the ledge again with both hands. With a jerk, he bent at the waist, kicking his feet up over his head, and propelled himself feet-first into the shaft onto his stomach, barely avoiding the robot's second pass below.

The sound of the blasting had stopped. But the explosions and electric eruptions only intensified. Jett not only had to escape the robot, but also this building before it went up in flames.

Reaching the hatch, he put his hands to the big round wheel at the center of the door and strained. Nothing. It was stuck.

Behind him he could hear *clank, clank, clank*. The robot was making its way along the ledge toward the opening. More intensely this time, Jett strained at the wheel again. It still didn't budge. He listened—*clank, clank*. The robot was close.

"Oh, c'mon!" he wailed. "They never maintain these things like they should!"

He leaned back and roared in frustration, kicking the wheel with both feet, hoping to loosen the corroded mechanism. He grabbed the wheel with both hands and strained to turn it once more. With a deep *thunk*, it cracked open, letting in the cool nighttime air from the glass-domed environment outside.

There was a noise at the other end of the shaft. Jett quickly looked back. The robot was at the mouth of the tunnel, the paneled doors on its chest opening to release its fiery wrath once more.

Jett reached out and swung himself onto the service ladder that ran up the wall, just outside the hatch. A shower of blasts narrowly missed him as he clung to the ladder.

Explosions erupted behind him in the distance. The robot had struck several pallets of freeze-dried ice cream on the opposite side of the loading dock. Then, a frightful thought crossed his mind— if that robot got outside, continuing its reckless firing with those cannons, this whole section of the space port would be vulnerable.

Jett leaned over the hatch, being careful not to expose his hand to the opening, grabbed the door, and shut it, spinning the outside wheel to latch it tight. He looked around. He was on the opposite side of the building from the gash in the wall through which he had followed Frankie, three stories above the loading dock main deck. Jett looked up; his ladder extended two stories to the top of the roof.

He could hear clanking again. The robot was trying to make its way through the tunnel. He climbed up. Something had to be done to stop this relentless monster, but what? This robot was virtually unstoppable. If Jett had his gun, this all would be over with one shot. His ability with a pistol matched the legends of the gun-slingers of Earth's ancient Western times. But he knew that thinking in terms of *what if* and *could-have-been* was a waste of time.

Surveying the roof, Jett saw five large, randomly placed breaker boxes. Taking a closer look, he noticed that the one nearest the ladder didn't appear to be attached to anything—none of them did. Most likely, they were old discards from the room below that were replaced and had yet to be hauled away. They were all about the same size, about four feet high and five feet square.

The ranger studied the one nearest the ladder and thought for a moment. He walked around to the other side and pushed against it, testing its weight to see if he could move it. If only he could get it to the edge of the roof.

It was heavy and took all the strength he had left in his legs just to scoot it a little each time, but it was moving. If not for the lower gravity of the moon, he probably wouldn't have been able to move it at all. Inhaling deeply, he pushed with all his might as he slowly exhaled. He repeated this a few times until the breaker box finally eased up next to the ledge, when he heard the service door below open.

The robot had crawled its way through the tunnel. While it was in the process of pulling itself through the hatch, it rotated its head all the way around to see what was making the loud, metallic screeching sound from the roof above—just in time to witness its own decapitation.

With a booming crash that echoed through the girders of the dome, the breaker box hit bottom, smashing the robot's head to the floor. Peering over the edge, Jett saw the headless metallic body of the robot of death fall to join the scrap heap below.

He sighed deeply. The ranger leaned back, placing the palms of his hands flat on the roof behind him, and straightened his legs. He was hoping for a moment to relax, but instead, the hair on the back of his neck slowly stood on end as he realized the evacuation sirens were blaring in the distance. He had been too preoccupied with the robot to notice them before.

"Oh, great," he breathed.

The roof was warm from the fires that had started below. Soon it would become a blazing inferno if drastic measures weren't taken to extinguish it. He knew this was the reason for the sirens, which gave him a sinking feeling deep in the pit of his gut.

This space port was constructed as a cluster of conjoined glass domes, reinforced and supported by a giant spiderweb of iron girders and cross-members. In contrast to most edifices on Earth, erected to keep the environment out, this structure was designed to keep its environment in, with the extreme exception of uncontrollable fire.

Soon, the three large corridors that connected this dome with its surrounding cousins would be closed off by massive, downward-sliding gates, forming an airtight seal. Then, giant louvered vents at the dome's summit would open, purging all its gaseous contents like an immense boiling teakettle into the vacuum of space. The fire, having no more oxygen for fuel, would be extinguished.

Two minutes. That was the duration of the siren's call, enough time for everyone to move to the safety of one of the surrounding domes before the gates were shut. Two minutes from start to finish.

But Jett hadn't noticed when these wailing trumpets of doom began. He was probably still in the building when they started.

The sirens stopped. The silence seemed deafening.

Seconds later, the clanking of gears began the process of ratcheting down the monolithic barriers that would soon seal his fate.

Fatigued and dripping with sweat, he exhorted his body to perform one last time. The nearest exit was a good one hundred yards away to his right and five stories below.

He breathed deeply, then shot off in full sprint across the top of the building, running along the edge that dropped off to his left. Reaching the far corner, with a desperate grunt, he jumped.

In a diving leap, he stretched and gripped a chain hanging from a crane near the building. With a rasping sound of increasing speed, the ranger plunged five stories to the deck a little faster than he was comfortable with.

He hit bottom, tumbled, then jumped to his feet. Immediately, he went back down, grasping his right ankle with both hands. Sprained. He looked to his exit. The opening was less than half open.

In a galloping limp, he rushed to a flatbed cargo transport parked next to the wall. The ranger threw himself onto the buggy and mashed the accelerator, causing the car to careen sharply into the building next to it.

A loud *smack* was followed by the sound of screeching metal upon metal as the car ran alongside the structure. Overcompensating, Jett jerked the wheel back to the left, causing the buggy to go up on two wheels, almost tipping over. Correcting his course, the buggy came down and started rocking back and forth, almost bucking the ranger from his precarious mount. With a few quick, subtle maneuvers of the wheel, he finally had control and headed straight for his exit.

Jett wasn't sure there was enough time left. The gate was already lower than the height of the steering wheel. The buggy wouldn't make it through. He pressed harder against the accelerator, already to the floor, willing the transport to move faster. His vision became tunneled. The only thing that mattered to him was being on the other side of that gate when it closed. He watched it slowly slide down, like a giant cleaver. Would it be his sheltering refuge or an executing guillotine?

Fast approaching the diminishing gap, he gave the wheel a hard jerk to the left, sending the buggy into a sideways flip, throwing him to the ground in a violent tumble toward the opening. He stopped rolling, jerked his legs in, and pulled his arm close. His sleeve caught on the bottom of the descending gate as it clamped shut.

Inches from the now airtight seal, Jett lay pinned to the floor by his shirt as he heard the buggy smash into the door—on the other side.

A quick rumble followed by instant silence announced the purging of Zone 3. With a deep breath and a long sigh, the ranger closed his eyes and relaxed, savoring the much-appreciated moment of rest.

CHAPTER TWO

THE SHADOW

Captain Jethro Rogers stood erect, arms crossed, contemplating his recent activities on the moon. Failure to finally capture the small-time gangster, who once again slipped through his fingers, ignited a burning frustration within him.

He was alone in the clear, oval-shaped lift, swiftly propelling him upward along the outer shell of the tall, mirrored building. A crescent moon was still visible in the warm glow of Earth's early dawn, smiling at him mockingly, like an invisible Cheshire cat.

Like a forest of glass-covered monuments reaching to the sky, the city of Metropolis stood as a testament of man's crowning achievements in many things. The bustling activity below, in the city that never seemed to sleep, was transitioning between its nocturnal and morning shifts. The ground-level streets seemed to move as flowing rivers that washed through shadowy canyons between skyscrapers as a multitude of hover-cars made their way to their destinations. Hundreds of feet above the city's floor, the freeway system snaked its way through man-made canyons like suspended spiderwebs of steel and concrete.

The ranger withdrew the small piece of circuit panel he stripped loose from the debris of the killer robot that attacked him the night before and studied it again, slowly turning it over. He hoped someone at Ranger Headquarters would be able to explain the mystery of where it could have come from. He glanced out the turbo-lift window, the sun highlighting his reflection in the glass.

The public transit system was nearly at full capacity. Trains of cigar-shaped passenger cars, magnetically propelled along through reinforced plexiglass tubes, seemed to pulse in perfect unison like giant artificial arteries sending life to the buildings they penetrated. Hanging monorail trams slinked gracefully through the air, each egg-shaped cabin with its round porthole windows individually swinging out in succession as they swiftly rounded tight corners. The rest of the sky was filled with personal flying vehicles that seemed to swarm like gnats on a hot summer day.

The turbo-lift slowed to a stop as it approached the top floor of the five-hundred-story Space Ranger Headquarters Building. As Jett stepped into the lobby, he was met with the metallic greeting of, "Good morning" in a voice mostly monotone but still somewhat polite.

"If you say so, H-13," the ranger responded dryly as he walked past the short, squatty, robot busily polishing the floor. It was scooting back and forth on a round rotating brush, spun by a motor that made up the bottom half of its orange body. A glint of light flashed on a small, chrome emblem on its torso that read

"Hoover."

"Thank you," came the ill-fitting, programmed response from the janitorial machine, dutifully going about its cleaning.

Captain Rogers walked with a slight limp toward the door of the director's office.

"Good morning, Captain Rogers. Welcome back," said the eloquently spoken, nickel-plated android secretary sitting behind the desk. "Go on in; they're waiting for you."

"Thank you, Maria."

Captain Rogers was not particularly looking forward to this meeting with the director and assistant director of the Space Ranger Corps. It was not often that he returned from an assignment empty-handed. This time, all he had to show for months of tracking Frankie Malone was a sprained ankle and the small piece of circuit panel in his pocket.

The automatic door slid open in front of Jett, revealing a man standing with his back facing the exit, still speaking at the director. It was Rupert Praxton, chairman of the newly formed oversight committee of the Space Ranger Corps. He was a bureaucrat through and through, an expert at the conducting of public affairs for private advantage. For him, the appearance of procedure was more important than outcomes. His first priority was always himself. Naturally, Jett did not like the man.

"... and remember, we have elections coming up soon. This type of reckless stuff has to stop," barked the chairman, wagging his finger at the director. "I'm in charge of funding for this department, and that includes recommendations for its structure, if you know what I mean."

Rupert Praxton took a step to leave, then turned back abruptly and pointed. "I mean it, this needs to be taken care of, and soon!"

The bureaucrat spun to leave so fast that he almost ran into Jett, who was standing just behind him.

"How do you do, sir?" Jett extended a hand.

"I do what I have to," replied the chairman, and shook the ranger's hand while walking out, not even looking at him. He didn't show his glowing smile today; he never did when the cameras weren't around.

"Oh, good morning, sir. How do you do?" said a tepid Brack Tellerson, trotting to the exit after Praxton. He quickly produced a hand, and Jett shook it too. The handshake was limp, cold, and clammy, like grabbing a dead fish. Tellerson was a rotund man, always hiking his pants up in the rear. He was once a governor, but now running for the Senate; he and Praxton were both cut from the same cloth.

As soon as the two men left, Jett wiped his hand on his pants leg and crossed the spacious room toward the director's desk, which sat in front of a colossal wall-to-wall, floor-to-ceiling fish tank.

The tank did double duty, also being the window that looked out to the city of Metropolis, giving the wonderful and surreal illusion of the aquatic creatures inside swimming through the air along with the flying vehicles passing by outside.

Sitting on the edge of the desk, one leg dangling, was the assistant director. He had an easy way about him and always seemed to have a friendly smile on his face. "Hello, Jett."

"Good morning, Assistant Director Handrix," replied Captain Rogers.

Jett's eyes centered on the hunched figure of a large man, arms crossed and elbows resting on the desk. "Good morning, Director Freder," said Jett with a polite nod.

"Jethro," responded the grim-faced director, in a deep, guttural voice and slight Hungarian accent.

He was an intimidating-looking man. His eyes seemed to burn with a piercing intensity, suspended in a sea of sunken shadows created by the ridge of his brow. His hair had the appearance of white flame as its upward-twisting locks glowed from the iridescent light passing through it from the fish-tank window behind.

Sitting in a chair near the director's desk was an attractive young woman with short, light-brown, wavy hair, in Space Ranger attire.

Before Jett reached the desk, the young woman stood and introduced herself. She stuck out her hand and, with a curt smile, said, "Betty Warren."

"Jett Rogers. Nice to meet you," he responded, shaking her hand.

"It's nice to meet you too. In the academy, I included in my thesis your apprehension of the Jekari Gang of Jupiter's Gamma-5 district. Well … actually it was just a side bar note." She wrung her hands. "But anyway, I thought the way that you tricked them into trapping themselves in that abandoned Usidium mine was brilliant."

"Well, I hope you didn't give me all the credit," said Jett with a nonchalant chuckle. "It was kinda just an accident that it turned out that way. I don't know that I'd call their apprehension 'brilliant,' but I appreciate the compliment just the same."

After giving her a quick smile, Jett turned to face the director, when the assistant director started into him. "You sure made a mess of things this time. And an expensive one at that! For cryin' out loud, Jett, it's gonna take at least a month for them to get that power plant repaired and operational again. This is very sloppy work for a ranger. Even for *you*!"

"Wha … now hold on. I can explain," said Jett, defensively.

"And the clean-up that's involved! Good gravy! The whole facility in that section was completely destroyed. They're just starting the removal process up there now as we speak," continued Handrix.

"Does this have anything to do with those snakes that were just in here?" Jett jerked his thumb toward the door.

"Don't worry about them. We'll take care of that," replied Handrix.

"I'm telling you, though, it's not my fault. I had …" Jett was cut off again, this time by the deep voice of the director.

"I also hear that you lost your gun. Again."

"There's an explanation for that too, if you'll just …"

"You checked out a new one this morning. Are you starting a

collection?" The director seemed to stare straight through him.

Jett paused for a moment, feeling deflated. He was carrying a new gun, but the director knew that it was another replacement. He also knew it was futile to argue with the director. He reached into his pocket, pulled out the piece of circuit-panel, and placed it on the desk.

"*This* is what caused the damage," said Jett pointedly. "It's from a robot that was equipped with rapid-fire laser cannons. They were hidden in a compartment in its chest." He waited for Handrix to pick it up. "Do you recognize these markings, over here on the edge?" He pointed.

Jett's two superiors became silent as they marveled at the circuit-panel with its strange, alien markings. As Jett stood in front of the desk, watching them examine this new piece of evidence, his mind turned to Betty. Who was she, and why was she here? He thought this meeting was going to be just between the director, assistant director, and himself, to discuss Frankie Malone's escape. He hated to make mistakes and rarely did. But when things went wrong for Captain Jethro Rogers, they were usually big. He always dreaded the reprimand that was sure to follow. But today, to add insult to injury, there was this strange woman standing quietly by as his audience.

A large, helium-filled zeppelin passed by, just outside the fish-tank window. It was a tourism ship that gave sight-seeing excursions of the city from above. The image of the magnificent, slow-moving vehicle crossing the window appeared like a giant whale attempting to feed on the smaller fish it pursued.

With an ominous voice of ill-boding, the director spoke. "This is very interesting and rather disturbing, but you're going to have to let Frankie Malone go for a while. You're getting a new assignment, Jethro."

The assistant director handed Jett a folder marked TOP SECRET. OPERATION DARK MATTER.

Jett opened it and quickly shuffled through the papers until he came to some crime scene holographic photos that depicted three separate, gruesome murders.

"How strange," said Jett. "Their clothing ... they almost look like ranger uniforms."

"Not almost," Handrix replied grimly. "They are."

Although it happened from time to time, it was rare to hear of a ranger being killed in the line of duty, especially during this current time of relative peace in the solar system. But Jett had never heard of anything like this happening since the time his grandfather was in the corps. That's what made the holographic photos seem almost unbelievable.

With a troubled voice, Jett uttered, "This really *is* a dark matter." He turned to Handrix. "Who were they, and how did this happen?"

"Captains Mason and Conroy and Major Gordon," replied the assistant director. "We're not sure how this happened, or even why."

"What information do we have so far?" asked Jett.

Handrix shook his head disparagingly. "None. That's why you're being reassigned to this, Jett. All we know so far is that this must be the work of a single assassin." He pointed to the holographs, indicating the obvious similarities in each victim's death. "The one connection between the three rangers is that each was investigating illegal weapons trafficking in the Martian sector."

Jett spread the holographic photos out on the director's desk and stood shaking his head, still in disbelief. Each ranger had been gruesomely carved into many pieces, similar to a sausage link crudely run through a deli slicer. It wasn't uncommon to see images depicting heavy doses of gore come through the offices of the Ranger Corps. As a matter of fact, it was all too common. But when it concerned rangers themselves, especially with this level of sadistic cruelty, that was something entirely different.

"These were all good men," Jett said. "Very experienced and extremely capable. Top of the line—no one would dispute that. A single assassin did this to some of the best rangers in the corps?"

"This is your new assignment, Jethro," said Director Freder. "Take your new partner and bring in this assassin, so we can find out who's behind this." His hand was outstretched for Jett's. He took it, shook it hard, and let go. Strangely, Jett thought he detected a sort of farewell in it.

"If you will all please excuse me," said the director. "I have to leave for another meeting."

Out of the corner of his eye, Jett glanced at Betty. She returned a quick smile.

He waited for the door to close behind the director, then launched at Handrix.

"Did I hear that correctly? He did say *partner*?" Jett jabbed his thumb in Betty's direction. "*Her*? If this is some kind of joke"—he pointed his finger at Handrix—"I would think this is a highly inappropriate time."

The assistant director shrugged apologetically, "I'm sorry Jett, but the director's made up his mind. There's nothing I can do."

"Are you sure the chairman isn't pulling these strings? This sounds exactly like the type of idea that an inept bureaucrat would come up with."

"You've always been allowed a certain latitude to speak freely because of your position, Jett," said Handrix. "But you're treading on thin ice in this current environment, so I'm going to advise you to be careful what you say."

"These politicians," replied Jett, "always talking about 'progress' when they're constantly getting in the way. And another thing," he continued. "Whatever happened to the idea of 'one case, one ranger'? If you don't think I'm doing my job well enough, you can always get someone else, sir."

"It has nothing to do with that, Jett, I assure you," replied Handrix. "I know this is a bit unique, but this is how it's going to be. I would introduce the two of you, but it seems you've already met."

Forehead wrinkled and nostrils flared, Jett turned to Betty. "Just how much experience do you have anyway?"

Betty felt somewhat threatened and answered with a rather impish voice, "J-just finished the academy."

Jett turned and glared at the assistant director. "You're not giving me a partner. You're making me a baby-sitter."

Handrix glanced down to his shoe, raising his eyebrows in another apologetic gesture. "I told you, its outa my hands."

Turning on his heel, with fists and teeth clenched, Jett marched straight for the door and grumbled to himself, "Great!"

———

An uncomfortable silence between them, Jett and Betty stood, gazing out through the turbo-lift glass, as it descended to ground level. Each of them pondered their own questions of this unlikely pairing and intentionally avoided eye contact with the other.

What was the director thinking? thought Jett. It was unprecedented for a field-ranger to have a partner, especially one so green. All she could possibly do was slow him down.

The young female ranger nervously stole a glance at the man standing beside her, the man that she was told would be her partner on her first assignment just earlier this morning. She was thrilled about the opportunity of working with such an accomplished ranger as Captain Rogers. Even though he was still relatively young himself, his achievements rivaled many of the most seasoned veterans. Her feelings of recent excitement were now replaced with doubt and uncertainty. His protest of her in the director's office made her feel like an unwelcome shadow.

The turbo-lift door opened. They walked through the main lobby and stood outside, atop the steps that, like a broadening waterfall, cascaded down to the street below.

"If you don't mind me saying, Captain Rogers, even though you're not so keen on the idea … um, well, it's a privilege for me to get to work with you." Betty flashed a weak smile, shuffling her feet.

He glanced at her, reached into his pocket, broke off a small piece of jerky, grunted, and began chewing.

She frowned.

A sleek metallic-silver hover-car caught Jett's attention as it drove past. It had the new gull-winged top-opening doors and sporty split rear window. The driver looked strangely familiar.

"What?" the ranger whispered unconsciously. It took a moment for him to realize that it was Frankie Malone.

"It's him!"

"It's who?" asked Betty.

"What's he doing here?"

"What are you talking about?"

"Quick! Get in the car!" Jett hobbled down the steps as best he could with his sprained ankle.

"Which one?" Betty hurriedly followed Jett as he swiftly descended the steps flapping his arms like an injured duck, trying to keep most of his weight on his good leg.

Jett jumped into his car and fired up the engine.

Betty blinked hard. "What is *that*?" she blurted. It looked like something she had only seen in a museum. This vehicle didn't hover, it sat, planted firmly to the street on what seemed like rubber tires. Its long, cigar-shaped body, positioned between four fenderless wheels, was coupled to the chassis with an intricate, crab-like suspension. It had a round, wood-handled steering wheel and pleated red leather seats that sat low in the open cockpit, two-thirds of the way toward the back. It was painted a deep chocolate brown, with six chrome pipes on each side, extruding horizontally from the engine compartment in the front and gathering in one larger pipe below that ran the distance of the chassis to the rear.

Betty climbed into the passenger side. "What are we doing?"

"Just hang on!"

With a push of the clutch and shifting of gears, they darted into the stream of traffic. By the sound of its fearsome rumble and catlike quickness, despite its antique outward appearance, the car had some definite modern modifications.

After navigating his way over to the far-right lane, Jett turned to Betty. "Do you see that silver car up there, just now turning?" She responded with a nod. "It's the thug, Frankie Malone. A small-time gangster I've been tracking for over a month. He's either extremely bold or profoundly stupid showing his face so near Space Ranger Headquarters. After all this time, I still don't know who he's working for. I'm gonna follow 'im and see where he goes. Maybe

I'll finally be able to put this case to bed."

"I thought you were just taken off that case," said Betty.

"Yeah, you're right, but who am I to look a gift horse in the mouth?" he replied coolly.

She sat back, adjusting her posture against the supple leather seat, and surveyed the interior of this relic of an automobile from a bygone era. The gearshift was a slender chrome shaft, tipped with a round ivory knob. The instrument panel, set in an oval-shaped cove in the dash, was a cluster of round chrome-trimmed, black-faced, needled gauges.

The ride was much smoother than she expected from a car that rolled along the pavement. The gradual up-and-down sensation of the suspension adjusting to the contour of the road and the breeze spilling over the windshield, wisping the top of her hair, she found therapeutic and relaxing. She fixed her eyes on the silver car ahead and began to wonder just what this day had in store for her.

"I've been in pursuit of this guy for months," Jett began. "Frankie had started out as a typical thug errand boy for bosses of the local criminal element of this sector. Technically, he's small potatoes, as far as gangsters go, hardly any real gang to call his own, and not too bright as a leader, but he's willing to get his hands dirty. This willingness to do anything allowed him to aggressively work his way up through the ranks, eventually rubbing elbows with 'bigger fish' within the dark underbelly of the solar system's syndicate."

Jett ran a red light to keep up, waved apologetically to the vehicle he cut off, then continued. "His connections alone could topple a great many dominoes within the organization."

As far as Jett was concerned, Frankie was the key that would unlock many doors. This particular mobster was like a greasy pig, though, always finding a way to slip through the ranger's fingers at the last moment. But this time, Jett thought, he was about to finally catch his prey.

———

Parked at the edge of a shadowed alleyway, they sat and watched Frankie from across the street. He exited his car, looking around constantly, as he entered the old movie theater on the corner. It was an ancient building from a more romantic time that had been painstakingly restored to its original glory and was used to show films from early cinema. It was a beautiful structure, with its awning of a thousand light bulbs protruding over the sidewalk and its flashy, vertical neon signage that read *The Majestic*. Currently showing was a French silent from early science fiction: "*Le Voyage Dans La Lune*," read the marquee.

A Trip to the Moon. How ironic, thought Captain Rogers.

As soon as Frankie disappeared through the doors, Jett hastily said to Betty, "Let's go."

Entering the theater, their eyes adjusted to the dimly lit room as the light flickered from the projection on the screen ahead. They could see the silhouette of Frankie seated up front having a conversation with a creature that very obviously was not human.

Jett motioned for Betty to take a seat. They sat together, a short distance from the aisle, in the darkness of the back of the auditorium, watching in silence the conversation between Frankie and the mysterious creature.

Shortly, Betty leaned over and whispered, "Who is he talking to?"

"That's what I'd like to find out," Jett replied dryly.

"Do you know what kind of species that is?" she continued in a hushed whisper.

"One I've never seen before."

"What do you suppose he's doing here in Metropo ..." Before she could finish her sentence, Jett embraced her tightly and firmly planted a long, strong kiss on her lips.

The offended young woman struggled unsuccessfully against this highly inappropriate pass. She failed to notice that the conversation up front had ended; Frankie Malone had risen from his chair and started up the aisle straight for them. The only thing Jett could think to do, without blowing their cover, was to turn his back to the aisle and make it appear as if he and Betty were just another couple sharing a romantic moment.

Betty was finally able to break away. With a hard smack, she slapped Jett across his face. But not before Frankie had already left the room. Jett turned to the front; the mysterious creature was gone.

"*What* do you think you're doing!" Fists clenched and eyes

afire, she protested with a harsh and quite agitated voice.

"Come on, he's getting away." The ranger swiftly moved toward the aisle, rubbing his cheek.

Confused, still trying to assess exactly what just happened, she reluctantly followed.

Frankie turned from the concession stand, after purchasing a small box of cinnamon candy, and saw the two rangers emerge from the dark auditorium. Like a cat realizing it had just jumped off the fence into the dog pound, Frankie bolted.

"He's seen us!" Jett dashed, limping across the lobby and through the exit. The two rangers watched the silver hover-car furiously dart into the street and begin weaving its path through traffic.

"He's *not* getting away again! Come on!" Jett yelled, running for his car.

With the roar of an angry lion, the engine of Captain Rogers' car came to life, simultaneously sending all four tires into a piercing cry of screaming rubber and smoke. Betty felt the seat push into her back with an acceleration so strong, it took a moment for her to catch her breath.

The race was on. Zigzagging in and out of the moderately paced flow of traffic, the bellowing squall of the high-pitched, revving engine echoed through the glass canyons of Metropolis, coming back to them like a chorus of raging demons, as Captain Rogers shifted through the gears. The knuckles on Betty's fingers were turning white as she tightly squeezed the hand-grips beside the seat. They were traveling at dangerously excessive speeds she had never thought possible for a car.

Left hand firmly gripping the wheel, his right aggressively massaging the shifter between each gear change, Jett, with a determined focus, never took his eyes off the goal, far ahead. They passed through the traffic around them so rapidly that everyone else seemed to be moving in reverse. Gradually, they were gaining on the desperately driven fugitive.

Frankie turned a hard left, cutting across two lanes of traffic, causing a pile-up of five automobiles that had tried to avoid hitting him. He had entered an on-ramp that swooped upward to the suspended freeway system, hundreds of feet above the city floor. With a down-shift and a quick acceleration through the turn, Captain Rogers continued the pursuit.

As they rocketed upward, hugging the curve of the winding expressway, Betty's breath became choppy, and the palms of her hands began to sweat.

The ranger's car, with its rubber tires, had a distinct advantage in the high-speed chase. Even though the rubber would sing with squeals of a slight skid, the ranger's car would dig in and slice through each curve with exact precision as they rounded each corner of the perilous slalom.

Frankie, on the other hand, was throwing sparks left and right as he rode the guard rails through each curving bend in the road. The anti-gravity responsible for keeping the hover-car off the ground allowed for much sway in the high-speed turns.

Betty glanced at Jett, hoping to catch a look of composed confidence on his face, reassuring her that they weren't going to die. Just then, she saw his look of grim determination relax, then contort into one of disbelief.

She snapped her attention back to Frankie. At the bottom rear of the silvery hover-car, two round apertures opened, revealing the orange glow of igniting rocket thrusters. With an exceptional boost of speed, the car catapulted forward, burst through the guard rail, and went over the edge.

Jett stood on the brake, locking the tires and sending his car into a screeching skid, right up to the edge where Frankie had gone over.

Jett and Betty peered over the side to see what had become of Frankie. He had landed in an open boxcar of bundled soft goods on a flying freight train, about twenty cars long, that was passing just underneath them.

"That man's *crazy*!" said Betty breathlessly.

The last car of the train was just clearing the expressway as it slinked between the buildings, hundreds of feet above the city's floor. Once again, Frankie was getting away.

Jett glanced back over his shoulder; another train similar in length was approaching, following the path of the first. With a rev of the engine and a squeal of the tires, the car took off in reverse some distance back down the expressway before they came to a stop. Jett had his neck cocked, looking back and down over the ledge, and appeared to be counting quietly to himself.

Curious, Betty stretched her body and extended her neck to look over the side at what Jett was looking at. With disbelief and horror, she planted herself in the seat and grabbed Jett by his shoulder. "You're not *seriously* thinking about ...!"

Tires screamed once more as they launched forward. Betty swallowed hard. She remembered the excitement she felt when she was first informed that she was going to be Captain Rogers' partner, but she never dreamed the level of danger would be anything like this. If she could go back in time to make that choice again, she would have taken it all back. Betty's scream could be heard from a mile away as they flew off the side of the expressway. "We're gonna d-i-i-i-e-e-e-e-e!"

There was an empty flatbed car that seemed such a tiny moving target. Everything seemed to move in a blurring flash and in slow motion, all at the same time. With a thud followed by screeching rubber, Captain Rogers successfully landed the car. Their momentum would have carried them right over the side if the right-front tire had not come to rest against the support rail at the front end of the platform. The left-front wheel was precariously hanging off the edge.

Jett peered over the side at the dangling tire, exhaled deeply, and wiped the sweat from his brow. He quickly changed his expression and turned to Betty with a slight arrogant smirk. "So, how do you like your first day on the job so far?"

She just glared at him with a disapproving scowl, unable to say a word.

————————

The morning had become early afternoon, and the sun was high in the brilliant blue sky. Pillowy patches of clouds appeared as a scattered forest canopy of white, strewn through trees of glass, as the tall buildings grew upward through them.

The chase was momentarily on auto-pilot as they waited for the trains to reach the warehouse district on the outskirts of the city. Frankie Malone would be surprised. He would not have expected the ranger to attempt such a daring stunt on the freeway overpass.

Jett kept his eyes on the train far ahead that was carrying his elusive fugitive. Betty sat quietly, looking down at the ground below that was now rising up to them as the trains began their descent. Large banners were being erected across the streets below for the annual Memorial Festival, which was still a few days off.

As the first train pulled up alongside the loading dock, the supervisors of the worker robots stood dumbfounded as they watched the silver hover-car come barreling down from atop the heap.

The second train pulled in behind the first one. Frankie gazed in his rear-view mirror in disbelief as he watched the ranger's car drive off onto the loading dock. Through the warehouse and down a ramp, they emerged from a large, hangar-type doorway in the rear of the building onto a ground-level alleyway. The chase resumed.

Frankie Malone flew through intersections with reckless

abandon, narrowly escaping several collisions. The rangers followed, weaving their way through the sequential pile-ups that Frankie had left in his wake.

Frankie barely squeezed through a busy intersection just after the signal turned red and the cross traffic began to go. Determined not to lose sight of the silver car ahead, Jett jammed his car down into a lower gear. The ranger's car whined a high-pitched scream as he mashed the accelerator to the floor.

Betty closed her eyes tight and gritted her teeth. Approaching a sharp dip in the road before the intersection, the car crouched, then sprang up as it hit the dip like a ramp, soaring through the air over the crossing traffic, barely clipping a plastic sign on a delivery truck's roof with its back tires. With a violent jolt, the car landed, and the pursuit continued.

Frankie rounded a corner a little too wide and clipped the edge of a new radio transmission tower. A large metal sign dislodged from above and fell to the side of the road, just as Jett's car sped past. The sign read "GISMO Robotics. Under Construction."

The traffic eventually became sparse as they raced down a major thoroughfare leading away from the city. As the curving road gradually opened up to a long straightaway ahead, Jett reached down and turned a nozzle on a cylinder under the seat. A small button atop the gearshift knob was engaged, sending the mixture of high-performance fluid from the cylinder to the engine. The tires squealed with renewed vigor, and the car shot off like a bullet. With the leather seat pressing more firmly into her back every moment, Betty stole a glance at the instrument panel. The speedometer, which read up to a 170 miles per hour, was forcing the pegged needle hard against its limit.

As Metropolis became a small speck on the horizon in the distant rear, trees and grass became more infrequent as the landscape transitioned from lush green to desert. They were now on the open road and swiftly gaining on the criminal.

Jett yelled to Betty through the rushing wind of the open cockpit, "Use your laser pistol, and see if you can hit his car!"

"I don't have one!" she yelled back, fighting to keep her hair out of her face.

"*What!*"

She stewed. "I just graduated from the academy and haven't been issued one yet! I was supposed to pick up my gun this morning after we left headquarters, but we started this crazy chase of yours *first!*"

After a short pause, he gave a nod of concession. "Here, use mine!" He handed her his new pistol.

Her first few shots went slightly astray as she adjusted herself to the wind and movement of the car. Then, she grazed his right fender. After one final adjustment, she sent a blast through Frankie's rear window, narrowly missing him. All rangers are well-trained marksmen, and Betty was no exception.

"Don't kill 'im!" shouted Jett. "I need to question him!"

"I was just getting his attention! That *is* what you wanted, isn't it?"

Frankie cut a hard right, leaving a blinding trail of billowing dust as he barreled down an abandoned rural road.

Bringing his car down to a safer speed, Captain Rogers stuck with him like a bloodhound, relentlessly refusing to be thrown from the trail.

"I can't see!" Betty put her hand up to shield her eyes.

Jett reached behind the seat and pulled out two pairs of goggles. "Put this on!" The pair he gave Betty was attached to a soft leather hood.

The hover-car now had the advantage. The road was extremely rough, violently jostling the two rangers as they sped across the rugged terrain. Jett shouted over the noise. "Keep shooting at the car! See if you can disable it!"

She hesitated. "I ... I don't have it anymore."

Reluctantly, he responded, "What do ya mean?"

There was a long, uncomfortable pause. "Remember that giant pothole back there? It jarred me so hard, I dropped it."

"You *lost* my gun?" He glared at her.

She pathetically forced an apologetic smile.

"It was a really big pothole! I almost fell out!"

He jerked his gaze back to the road. "You should've!"

In the swirling haze of Frankie's trail, Captain Rogers began to notice boulders of increasing size and frequency, zipping past them in the blur. Up ahead, in the dusty fog, he could see the orange glow of rocket thrusters beginning to ignite, just as they had on the expressway. But instead of increasing the throttle to try to keep up, his instincts told him to stand on the brake. The ranger's car went into a sliding skid, not getting much traction at all in the loose dirt.

Through the dissipating dust ahead, they saw Frankie's car shoot over the edge of the cliff.

Captain Rogers' car was sliding too fast. They would not stop in time. Jett took his feet off the brake and, simultaneously popping the clutch, he threw the shifter into reverse and stood on the accelerator. Four rooster-tails of dirt and gravel spewed forward, and the desperate roar of the mighty engine could be heard echoing from the abyss below as it furiously compelled the all-wheel-drive to claw its way back to safety. The front of the car went over the edge and stopped, teetering, as the nose dipped downward.

An echo could be heard off the far wall of the canyon. "We're gonna d-i-i-i-e-e-e-e!"

The engine was still roaring, and the wheels were still spinning, vainly grasping at the air. The nose swung back up as the rear finally settled, giving the back tires traction once more. With a few vicious jerks, the car wrenched itself back away from the edge.

Jett and Betty both stood up in the car and leaned over the windshield to see what had become of Frankie. As the silver car grew smaller, plummeting to the dark abyss below, the gull-winged door opened. They saw a flash of orange with the hissing of jets.

Frankie had a strap-on rocket pack and, with the swiftness of a missile, was streaking upward toward them. Quickly approaching the precipice just below the two rangers, he swooped back out toward the center of the canyon, drawing a laser rifle.

"Get down!" shouted Jett. In their haste to quickly take cover, they bumped heads.

Frankie pelted the area with laser blasts as he made his escape in the opposite direction.

When the blasting finally stopped, Jett peeked over the dash, rubbing his forehead. Frankie was flying away, far into the distance. He sighed, "Oh, great."

Betty raised up, rubbing her forehead, and saw steam spewing from the car's radiator. The engine had been riddled with laser blasts. There was a long silence while Betty glanced back and forth between Jett and the spewing radiator. There was also a small trail of smoke rising from the communication radio under the dash. It had been fried from an electrical surge when the battery was hit.

"This is bad, right? What does this mean?" she finally asked, almost afraid of the answer she knew was coming.

"This *means* we walk," said Jett, unable to hide the frustration in his voice. He opened the trunk lid on the rear quarter-panel of the car and pulled out a dark-red poncho, which was basically just a small, square blanket with a hole in the middle to pull over one's head.

"It's going to get cold tonight."

"Tonight? What do you mean, tonight? It's still early in the day."

He looked straight at her and said, gravely, "Metropolis is about thirty miles that way. If we cut across the desert, don't take any breaks, and we're lucky, we just might make it back by tomorrow morning."

Her eyes widened. "Oh, great."

CHAPTER THREE

HAUNTED SPECTER

A chorus of wailing coyotes in the distance sang a lament for the two rangers as they slowly trudged their way homeward. It had been hours since the black curtain of night had fallen, revealing glistening, pinpoint locations of millions of systems beyond, which they used as a heavenly compass to navigate their course steadily northeastward.

The many hours and miles of pounding and grinding, walking across the harsh, barren terrain, had taken a toll on Captain Rogers' sprained ankle. The swelling and throbbing that gradually ensued had slowly decreased their progress to a virtual snail's pace. They had just crossed a shallow, dry creek-bed and were ascending the short rise to the other side.

"You need to rest for a while," said Betty.

Jett had his arm around her shoulder, leaning on her for a crutch. He winced. "I'll be O.K. Let's keep going."

Vainly, he tried to conceal the pain, but she could see it written on his face with every step. He was determined to keep going all night. His frustration from letting Frankie escape a second time and his resolve to finish what he had started would not allow him to stop. He seemed to have an unrelenting drive that possessed him. It was almost unnatural. Like he had something burning inside that he had to prove. Whether to the world or to himself, Betty could not tell.

"*I* need to rest," she said finally.

Jett considered her for a moment. He knew her statement wasn't totally for his benefit. She had been carrying a great percentage of his weight for the past three hours and was showing visible signs of fatigue.

"Alright. Let's see what's over this rise, just for grins. Then maybe we'll take a break."

The idea did sound good to him. They were both tired, hungry, and cold. Jett's poncho, which Betty was now wearing, wasn't enough to keep sufficiently warm in the desert night air, and they had finished the last of Jett's jerky long before nightfall.

Clumsily, they trudged their way up the short slope of loose dirt and gravel. Reaching the small summit, they both stood silently for a few seconds. On the next plateau, nestled among sparse clusters of wild brush and shrubbery, stood an old shack of a house. The faint hint of smoke rising from the chimney could be seen by the dim glow of a crescent moon. Hopefully, they would find a friendly welcome, refreshment, and possibly an invitation to stay the night. With somewhat renewed vigor, they pressed on toward this welcome sight of shelter.

"Betty," said Jett innocuously, "if I may ask, what makes someone like you join the Ranger Corps in the first place?"

"What do you mean, someone *like me*?"

"No offense. Just curious. Everyone has their own reasons."

After several moments of thoughtful silence, she answered, "I would assume my reason isn't too different from the reasons most others join. Some want to make a difference that counts. Some may be thrill-seekers, *see the system*, and all that. And others feel compelled to make sure that certain wrongs of the past don't get repeated."

"Which of those is your reason?"

"I guess you could say a little bit of all of them."

Jett glanced at her. "What *wrongs of the past* are you trying to avert?"

She thought quietly again while they walked through the short desert brush, the soft crunching of dirt and gravel under their footsteps the only sound.

Finally, a sense of restrained passion rose in her voice. "Every victim of a crime has the right to be legally avenged by the law and not just have their case swept under the rug and forgotten about. Some people think bad things always happen to other people, until it happens to them. Then they say, 'Someone ought to do something about that.' Well, I wanted to be a *someone* and not a *them*."

He realized that his throw-away question of idle chit-chat had unintentionally struck an emotional chord that was used to being well guarded. He was now curious, but as the shack drew near and he observed their surroundings with greater detail, he began to think instead of potential danger.

Who would be out here? It was seemingly out in the middle of nowhere, with no apparent road leading up to it. Few people would choose to live in a place of such extreme seclusion as this—those who would just prefer to avoid the company of others, and those who had dealings of dubious legality, that would rather avoid the attention of the law.

A small perimeter sensor, slightly protruding from the ground by their feet, activated and blinked red in warning after they passed.

Jett tugged Betty's shirt and said in a hushed tone, "Be on guard. Whoever's in there may have something to hide. There's the possibility they might be—"

The cool desert air beside them crackled as a laser blast shot past the two rangers, striking a mound of dirt just behind. They threw themselves face down, flattening against the sand.

"—*unfriendly!*" Jett spit dirt from his lips.

They peered over the rusted pile of scrap metal behind which they had taken cover.

Standing in the doorway of the old shack was the frail silhouette of an elderly man holding a laser rifle. With slurred voice, he shouted, "Who's-ss there?" He leaned his shoulder against the jamb of the doorway to help steady his balance.

Jett observed the old man intently. He seemed harmless enough. Just an old, reclusive hermit who had been startled by their intrusion.

"We mean you no harm! We're Space Rangers!"

Two more blasts flew over their heads.

"Rangerss!" the old man exclaimed, disgustedly, still slurring heavily. "No r-rangers w-welcome here! L-lee-me alone!"

Betty turned to Jett. "He's drunk as a skunk!"

They stared at each other for a long moment. Another blast came flying over the heap.

"Is there anyone else in there we can talk to?" Betty was convinced that any further attempt to try communicating with this inebriated man was futile.

"No! Now g-go away, or I'll sh-sh, I'll shh ... I'll fry your hide." The man staggered in the doorway. A look of agitated hostility frowned his shadowed face. He stood like a feeble, haunted specter, guarding his forbidden mesa.

Jett rolled over on his side and scanned the yard, looking for a way out of their situation. It was no good; they were pinned down behind the rubbish pile. He shuffled through the pile of junk, jerked out a piece of rebar, and motioned to Betty. "Try to get him to come over here."

Her eyes registered concern. "Jett, no. Don't hurt him." She wasn't sure of his intentions.

"Don't worry. Just disarming him."

As they were speaking, the intoxicated man stepped away from the house and with a tipsy march, laser rifle drawn, advanced on the two crouching rangers.

"Captain Rogers, look out!" Betty blurted, recoiling with a start.

Jett quickly rolled, then came up with the piece of metal, striking the gun under the muzzle and twisting it away, out of the old man's hands.

The old hermit stood frozen, as if caught in a daze. He was a tall, thin man, with long white hair and high cheekbones. He stared at Betty, his eyes seemingly a bit more alert than just before. With a cracked voice, he breathed, "What did you s-say?" He reeked with the stench of cheap wine.

The two rangers exchanged questioning glances.

"I'm sorry, what do you mean?" she responded hesitantly.

"The name." He looked at Jett. "What did sh-she call you?"

Jett gave an enfeebled shrug of his shoulders. "Captain Rogers?"

The old man's eyes became glossy; muscles in his face contorted, trying to restrain emotion. His brow furrowed, and his chin tightened as his lip quivered for just a moment. His knees went weak, and he lowered himself in front of Jett, who caught the old man and slowly went to the ground with him.

The old man put his hand on Jett's shoulder and inspected the ranger carefully, as if he were some long-lost precious item that had just been rediscovered.

He looked into Jett's eyes and with a feeble, tortured voice whispered, "Buck … you're alright. You've-ve come back." Then he embraced Jett and began to weep before passing out in his arms.

Betty sat back, dumbfounded, gazing in wonder at the two figures now huddled together. Jett's face had turned ashen as if he had just seen a ghost. His eyes held a blank stare.

Betty cocked her head and gave him a sympathetic look. "What is it?"

Jett sat quietly for a moment, still holding the old man, keeping him from falling over.

She leaned over and touched his shoulder. "Jett, are you alright?"

He took a deep breath and swallowed hard. "Buck was my grandfather's nickname. You know, like that guy in the comics. Some fellas, just foolin' around, started calling him that when he joined the corps because of his last name. Then after a while, it just stuck. His real name was Nate. He was a ranger too, y'know." He paused for a moment, his gaze lowered to the ground. "It was a long time ago. He was killed in action when I was just a boy."

———

Betty sat contemplatively on the old, time-worn couch, watching dancing shadows sway hypnotically across the wooden floor in the small living room of the old man's house. Jett placed two more logs on the fire crackling in the stone fireplace in front of them.

The house was a disheveled mess of jumbled heaps of trash,

dirty dishes, dirty clothes, and a few empty bottles of booze here and there. The only visible patches of floor were the trails that allowed passage between the muddled piles of discarded junk. The place was very sparsely furnished with a couch, on which Betty sat, and a small table with some chairs in the kitchen.

Jett had carried the old man in and placed him on his bed to sleep off his intoxication.

"What do you suppose he meant by what he said to you?" Betty finally asked, breaking the long silence.

Jett sat on the floor for a long while staring at the fire, then slowly shook his head. "I don't know."

She could see that he was clearly disturbed by the brief conversation, if you could call it that, between himself and the mysterious old hermit, who was now beginning to snore, unconscious in the next room.

She ventured another question. "Is it possible he actually knew your grandfather?"

He shrugged. "I really don't know what to make of it. I don't recall ever seeing this man before in my life. Hopefully we'll get some answers in the morning." He leaned back, clasping his fingers behind his head, and lay on the floor.

Pulling off the poncho, Betty folded it for a pillow and stretched herself on the old couch, kicking some trash off the end. She put her hands behind her head and sighed, looking around the dark, shadowy room. By now, the partially lit moon had risen high in the cool desert night and dimly shone through the curtainless window, giving a faint blueish outline to the objects splashed by its beam.

As she lay staring up at the ceiling, which was being gently massaged by the soft light from the fire, and listening to the popping and cracking of the wood as it burned, the events of this first day of her first assignment as a Space Ranger began to replay in Betty's mind: the awkward introduction; the treacherous car chase; the long desert hike; this mysterious old man; her new partner; and, she touched her fingers to her lips, his unexpected kiss in the movie theater.

Jett lay flat on the floor and tried for many hours to force himself to get some sleep. But it seemed that the harder he tried, the more difficult it was. He felt unsure about so many things. His thoughts kept circulating back to Frankie Malone, the old man, and the riddle of this questionable pairing with his new partner. He unconsciously fiddled with his wrist watch, the one he had inherited from his grandfather, as his thoughts gradually morphed into strange dreams and he eventually drifted off into deep slumber.

––––––––––

It was a cool, spring morning, and a six-year-old Jethro Rogers stood graveside at his grandfather's funeral. The air had a faint scent of rain in the distance, and sun rays periodically poked through the clouds. A small gathering of family and friends stood atop the grass-covered hill. A little too small, the young Jett thought, for such a great man as his grandfather. Where was the flag over the coffin? Where was the twenty-one laser blast salute that he had seen so often on the news viewerscope? An accomplished Space Ranger, his grandfather surely was deserving of these things too.

When the man up front finished talking, the funeral was over and everyone started to head back to their cars for a meal at his grandmother's house, when a loud clap of thunder seemed to explode overhead.

Only it wasn't thunder.

Five Venusian cruisers had illegally entered Earth's atmosphere and raced overhead in a perfect V formation. The two on either side veered off to the left and right. The center ship went full thruster and in an instant was vertical, until it disappeared into space within a matter of seconds, leaving the faintest vapor trail behind. The young Jett Rogers stood erect, at full attention, tears streaming down his cheeks. His grandfather's wrist watch, which was too big for the child at the time, hung halfway down his arm as he saluted the Venus fighters, as they paid reverent final respects to his grandfather.

It was then that Jett noticed the man standing across the way in a Space Ranger dress uniform. He hadn't noticed him before, but he was saluting also. He was the only other person who was saluting with Jett; everyone else was just gazing upward at the unexpected spectacle. At that moment the man glanced at Jett, smiled, and winked. He was tall, thin, and had long, straight, white hair and high cheekbones.

———————

With a jerk, Captain Rogers awoke. The pale light of dawn filtered into the dingy room. He felt a strange strength born of panic. The mysterious old man was now awake and sober, standing over him with the cold muzzle end of his laser rifle planted firmly to the side of Jett's neck.

A NEW OLD FRIEND

Jett's experience of having to sleep alone in dangerous places had trained him to sleep lightly and awaken at the slightest change in the surrounding environment. He had never been surprised by anyone like this before and was amazed at the old man's stealth in sneaking up on him.

"Who are you? And what are you doing in my house, Ranger?" The voice was steadier than the night before.

Jett lay motionless and rolled his eyes up toward the old man. "I reckon you don't remember much about last night."

By this time, Betty was awake, remaining still on the couch, but watching, ready to move.

"Refresh my memory, Ranger," the old man coolly replied.

Captain Rogers rubbed his eyes and yawned. He cleared his throat then rehearsed the story of their high-speed chase that left them stranded in the desert and the cross-country trek that subsequently led them to the old man's house. "We do apologize for the intrusion," he continued. "Even though we spoke briefly, you didn't exactly invite us in."

"Your condition last night didn't allow for much conversation either," interjected Betty, now siting up on the couch. "It was Captain Rogers who brought you in and placed you on your bed."

"Come again?" The old man took a step back. "Who are you?" He looked intently at Jett.

Jett sat up. "I'm Captain Jethro Rogers, and this is my"—he gestured a casual hand toward Betty—"*sidekick*, Betty Warren."

The old man stood, altering his glance from Betty to Jett for a few moments, then finally said, "Since when did the notoriously *lone* rangers start working as partners?"

"Yesterday," said Jett matter-of-factly.

The old man cradled his gun in his arms. "Jethro Rogers," he said, thoughtfully. "I can see the resemblance. So, you grew up and decided to follow in the footsteps of your granddad."

The old man turned, hung his laser rifle on the wall, and walked toward the kitchen. "The two of you must be hungry; won't you join me for some breakfast?"

Betty was quite hungry; her stomach growled as she stood. It had been at least twenty-four hours since her last real meal, and she was feeling rather weak. As the old man made his way to the kitchen, she looked around at the messy, garbage-piled interior of the old shack and began to feel uncertain about the quality of breakfast they would be offered.

"Y'all are lucky today. I still have a good supply of prune juice. Oh, and looky here, have some sardines left too," said the old man as he rummaged through the cupboard. "I'm out of mustard, though."

Betty frowned.

———————

They sat around a rickety wooden table in the kitchen, the unusual breakfast set before them. Jett finally asked the question that had been burning in his mind all night. "How did you know my grandfather?"

The old man put down his cup of prune juice and adjusted his posture in his chair. His face showed the wear of many years, and memory painted dark shadows under his eyes, but they were still keen and sharp.

"First of all," said the old man, "I think it would be proper for the host to finally introduce himself to his guests. It seems I've overlooked that little pleasantry, until now. Please forgive me. You must understand, I've become somewhat out of practice to receiving visitors out here. My name is Eloi Lightfoot. Your grandfather and I went through the academy together and joined the Ranger Corps at the same time. He was my best friend. Toward the end, he was one of the few I knew I could really trust. I trusted him with my life"—Eloi paused and sighed deeply—"and he trusted me with his."

Eloi stared blankly at the window. His gaze seemed distant, as if looking back across decades of time. His voice had a soft quietness, more of wisdom of years than frailty of strength.

Jett was anxious for Eloi to continue. "Toward the *end?*"

he prodded.

"There was a time when your grandfather and I were the top rangers in the corps," Eloi continued. "The corps wasn't nearly as big as it is now; it didn't need to be. Outlaws feared rangers. We had true respect back then. Not like today. Oh, there were small gangs here and there, but for the most part, the solar system was clean. It was back in February of '32. I was tracking the gangster kingpin, Xridåhn."

Betty had managed to eat only one sardine. The slimy, crunchy fish was pungent and disgusting. She held her nose and swallowed hard, then drank her entire glass of prune juice to wash it down. With a wrinkled nose, she pushed her can of sardines aside. As hungry as she thought she was, her appetite had left her.

"He had developed a powerful network of organized crime on some of the lesser populated planets of the system, plundering their resources." Eloi gestured with his hands spread apart. "Earth was the one he wanted most, of course. Its resources alone are worth more than all the other planets in the system put together. But the rangers kept foiling his attempts at control. He was pretty sly, but I was constantly on his trail, getting ever closer. I knew it was just a matter of time until he slipped and made a mistake, and that's all I would need. Several times I thought I had him for sure, and he would slip right through my fingers, undetected. It was as if he could disappear into thin air, like magic. And in a sense, that's exactly what he was doing ... until I discovered his secret."

Eloi folded his hands on the table and stared out the window into the yard. In the silence, the two rangers patiently waited for him to continue. The old man seemed finished with all he had to say, but the two were certain that he had left them hanging.

Jett shifted in his chair, uneasily. "His *secret*?"

"He was an Oltercian," replied Eloi, puzzled by the inquiry.

By the muddled look on Jett's face, Betty perceived that he didn't know what the old man was talking about either. Eloi raised another sardine, licked his lips and slowly began chewing it.

Betty raised her hand, sarcastically, and ventured the question that both she and Jett wanted to know. "Um ... what's an *Oltercian*?"

Eloi raised his glass to take a sip and halted midway. He stared at Betty, then at Jett. "You don't know?" They both quietly shook their heads.

"It was all in my report. Very detailed too, including my own sketches of the creature's appearance. Surely the account of the ambush and ranger massacre by Xridåhn's gang are required study at the academy."

"Yes, you're right," replied Jett, "but I've never heard of an 'Oltercian,' as you call it."

Eloi stared at the tabletop between them and thought out loud, "A mystery for sure. Why would that information not be included? I'm the only one who had any detailed knowledge of the being. Oh, uh ... except for your grandfather."

Betty pursed her lips, glanced sideways at Jett, then back to Eloi. "Sorry to keep coming back to this, but can you please tell us, *what* is an Oltercian?"

"Oh, yes," Eloi's attention snapped back to the present. "An Oltercian is a unique being. He has the unusual and rare ability to manipulate. To the best of my knowledge, there are no others left of their ancient race."

Still not understanding a word he was saying, no longer hiding her frustration, she wrinkled her face and quickly shook her head. "*What?*"

"Like a chameleon. He has the ability to change the color of his skin. But that's not the most impressive part." He leaned over the table toward them, his eyes got big, and he gestured with his fingers, his voice hushed. "By manipulating the muscles in his face and body, he can make himself look human, possibly up to as many as two, maybe even three different physical appearances. That's why he was so successfully elusive at first. The creature Xridåhn could walk into a building as one person and walk out as someone completely different. When I finally discovered his secret, we made plans to raid one of his hideouts where he was thought to be. Major Freder dispatched me to take charge of it."

"Director Rotwang Freder?" asked Jett.

Eloi frowned. "He's director now?"

"For about eight months," said Jett. "Director Adams before him was killed in a space cruiser accident."

"Adams?" Eloi said with a puzzled look. "What about Barton?"

"Director Barton died in his sleep, very suspiciously, two years ago. Reports suggested a sting-adder, but it was inconclusive since it happened on Venus. You know, interplanetary sharing of info is like pulling teeth."

Eloi stared blankly at the table top between them, thinking to himself and slowly shaking his head. "Hmmmm ... Director Freder. How times change."

"Go on," said Betty, "about the raid."

"We raided Xridåhn's hideout with eight rangers." Eloi slowly shook his head. "It should've been a cake-walk. But somehow, they were tipped off and knew we were coming. They were waiting in ambush. What a dark day in my memory. Seven of the very finest rangers were brutally murdered, including your grandfather."

"My grandfather?" asked Jett.

"Yes," sighed Eloi, "your grandfather. But not before he took out nine of those savage dogs himself. What a fighter. He was the best. I don't think there will ever be another like him.

"Politicians wanted to sweep it under the rug and pretend it never happened," continued Eloi. "They wouldn't even provide a proper, dignified funeral for them. The whole thing was so terribly mishandled, from start to finish."

"You were there," said Jett. "At the funeral."

"Yes ... I was the only survivor. The whole thing was so disgusting to me, how they treated us, that I walked away from the Ranger Corps soon after."

"I thought he was killed in an explosion," replied Jett. "That's what I've always been told."

"Politically explosive," said Eloi. "That's why they didn't want the real story to get out. They were afraid the truth would rattle the public's faith in the Space Rangers. But it was an ambush. The explosion story was manufactured. I'm sorry, kid."

"How did you get out?" asked Betty. "The ambush?"

"Oh!" Eloi leaped from his chair and trotted through the kitchen to his bedroom. He navigated rather gracefully along the narrow trail that divided the piles of rubbish. "I have something I think might be of interest to you," he yelled back. When sober, he could move almost like a cat, not making even the slightest sound on the creaky old floorboards of the house.

The two rangers watched the old man through the doorway of his bedroom; he heaved piles of trash from one side to the other, mumbling to himself. "O.K. now, where is it?" After moving nearly half the room around, he finally exclaimed, "Ah! Here it is!" A hidden trap door was raised from the floor in the corner of the room. He came walking back into the kitchen with an object in each hand.

"Here's a beautiful thing." He reached his right hand to Jett. "It was your grandfather's laser pistol. I think it's more appropriate that you have this now, rather than me. Especially seeing how, um, curiously, you go about your business as a ranger unarmed."

Jett glanced angrily at Betty and grabbed the pistol by the hand grip. It was heavier than his last, being a much older design—the

XZ-38 model—but the balance still felt perfect in his grip. The bronze coating had lost its luster with many years of tarnish, but the insulator rings near the muzzle, in front of the coil housing, were still gleaming as if new.

"And *this*," said Eloi with a proud grin, as he held out his left hand, "was his back-up."

Jett holstered his grandfather's pistol and held out his hand to take the object from Eloi. "What is this?" Jett inspected the tiny antique weapon.

"That, my boy," said Eloi, "is a Remington two-shot Derringer."

"How does it work?" asked Jett. "It looks like a toy. Where's the laser-coil?"

Eloi erupted in laughter. "It doesn't fire laser. It shoots bullets. This is an antique from the ancient times. Your grandfather had a certain affinity for those sort of things. His nickname fit his personality well. Be careful there; it's still loaded. I think he got it from some antique dealer."

"As long as you have a good blaster at your side"—Jett patted his grandfather's gun—"what good would something as dinky as this do?"

Eloi's giddy appearance became stern. Pointing his finger at Jett, he instructed, "A good ranger *always* has a back-up."

"How did you come to have these?" asked Jett.

"Your grandmother wanted me to have them, since your grandfather and I were close," responded Eloi. "But now it's time for them to move on, to someone more appropriate."

Jett frowned, considering the tiny two-shot pistol in the palm of his hand, then he turned and handed it to Betty. "Here, now you have a weapon. Try not to lose it this time."

"Oh, thank you," she said sarcastically, considering the statement coming from a man who, at least in the director's opinion, was notorious for losing his own. After examining it for a bit, she pocketed the small curiosity.

Jett pulled something from his pocket and placed it on the table. He had swiped the circuit panel from the director's desk before leaving. "What do you make of this? Have you ever seen anything like it?"

Betty crossed her arms. "You brought that with you? You never intended to leave that alone, even after the director reassigned you?"

Eloi picked up the panel and carefully studied it.

Jett paid no attention to Betty. "I'm especially interested in these markings over here on the side," he said to the old man, pointing.

"Where did you get this?" asked the old hermit.

"From a worker robot on the moon. It was equipped with rapid-fire laser cannons and tried to kill me. It left quite a mess, to say the least."

Eloi's eyes registered great concern. "Earth's moon?"

"Yes. What do you make of these markings?"

Cocking an eyebrow, Eloi said, with slight trepidation, "I think it's Martian. I can't say for sure though because of its cryptic nature, like high-level military or something … similar."

"Martian military, are you sure?" said Betty. "What is something like that doing on the moon?"

The old man casually wheeled around to her. "Well, I'm not sure it's Martian yet, but I think I know someone who can tell us."

"Where can I find him?" asked Jett.

"You won't," said Eloi. "But I can."

"I do appreciate the offer," said Jett, "but that will be unnecessary. I'm rather skilled as a tracker. If you could just tell me where to begin, that'll be enough."

"You don't understand." The old man shook his head. "This someone I know is very particular about who he associates with. I could send you to him, but he wouldn't tell you anything, if you were even able to find him. I'm the only ranger he trusts … will talk to, anyway. If you want to get any useful information out of him at all, you will have to take me along with you. Of course, it's your choice." He glanced at Betty. "You two seem to have something else that you're busy with right now anyway, so, maybe we should forget about it."

Jett looked around at the mess of a house and pondered how this old man could possibly help them. When he halted his gaze upon Betty, he realized that at this point he had nothing to lose by trusting the man. "Alright then, you win. Where are you taking us?"

"We will most likely find him on the space station Aurora Four, orbiting Neptune," said Eloi.

Jett stepped over to the screen door and peered out through the tattered mesh. "How soon can we leave?"

Eloi stood erect and brushed the wrinkles from his green flannel shirt. "Right away, I suppose. I just need to grab a few things."

"Captain Rogers," said Betty, "don't we already have an assignment? We've got to get to the bottom of what happened to … you know."

"Yes, I've not forgotten." Jett remained at the door and folded his arms to his chest. "Where, then, would you have us begin the investigation of these assassinations, Betty?"

"In the area where they took place," she said. "In the Martian sector."

He had inadvertently said more than he should about their current assignment by mentioning the assassinations. In his mind, Jett blamed the director more than himself. Having such a junior partner tag along was a real and potentially dangerous distraction. It's not that he disagreed with Betty, but he was accustomed to following his gut. And right now, the compass in his gut was pointing hard at finding the origin of this alien circuit panel first, especially now that he seemed to have a fresh lead.

"Yes, so would I," he replied. "So, on our way to the Martian sector, we'll stop off and question Eloi's contact. Believe me, I want to catch who's responsible just as badly as you."

"But this time of year," said Betty, "Neptune is in rotation almost completely on the opposite side of the sun from Mars."

"What assassinations?" Eloi had been standing by, curiously watching their debate, thinking to himself about the awkward unconventionality of two rangers being assigned to the same investigative mission. "What's this about assassinations in the Martian sector?"

Jett pressed his lips together tightly. He was reluctant but now felt compelled to let Eloi in on some of the details. After all, he was an ex-ranger, and Jett didn't want feelings of distrust to fester between them before they even shoved off. He described the horrors of the crime scene photos that he had been shown at headquarters the day before and the assignment he and Betty had been given to apprehend the murderer of the three rangers.

Eloi stood stoically, thoughtfully digesting the information. "The solar system is obviously not safe at this time for those who are supposed to be the stewards of peace. We should do our traveling in stealth. For the right fee, I know a place in Shangri-la where we can charter a ship. He's an old friend. Questions of our intentions will be kept to a minimum."

"That sounds like a good idea," said Jett. "We should leave at once then."

"Good." The old man disappeared into his room.

Betty stepped up beside Jett, tugged on his jacket sleeve, and whispered, "Are you sure about this? Putting our trust in someone we hardly know?"

"He's an ex-ranger," replied Jett. "Plus, he served with my

grandfather. In a way, he's sort of like a new old friend."

Eloi emerged from his room wearing leather lace-up moccasin-style boots, an old cross-holstered laser pistol, and a poncho similar to Jett's, except dingier and time worn. "Let's go." The old man marched out the front door.

Jett stood in the middle of the yard and considered the old truck Eloi was climbing into. It was a rusted, dilapidated mess of an old flatbed farm hauler, which looked as if, at one time, it might have been painted blue with red on the sideboards of the bed. Precariously sitting on four cinder blocks, it was shrouded in weeds, some of which were growing up through a rusted hole in the hood.

"That piece of junk will never run," Jett said to himself, as the old man turned the ignition. *Click*. Nothing.

"C'mon, ol' gal; you can do it!" they heard Eloi shout, as he banged on the dash and pumped the floor pedal.

Jett and Betty both gazed longingly in the direction of Metropolis. It was still a long walk away.

After several unsuccessful tries, Eloi raised the hood and attempted a few adjustments. "I'm not sure why it's not working," he said. "It worked fine the last time I drove it."

"How long was that?" asked Jett.

"Oh, only a couple of years ago, I think."

None of Eloi's attempts at fixing the engine seemed to work. Betty laid a hand on the fender and peered into the compartment.

"It looks like an early twelve-volt system," she said. "May I take a stab at it?"

"Sure, go ahead." Eloi raised his palms in mock surrender, then brushed them off. "Just don't break anything. This is my baby."

She couldn't help but give the old man a double take. "I'll be gentle."

Betty rearranged some wires, bypassing a few connectors that appeared to be fried. "Give it a try."

There was a shrill, screeching sound of metal upon metal. "Oh, my baby!" cried Eloi.

"Sorry about that." Betty raised a hand apologetically, head still buried in the engine. "One more adjustment." She cut two wires, spliced them together, then stood up. "O.K., try it again."

With a loud *snap* and a large plume of dark smoke, the ionic engine engaged.

The old truck was now hovering above the cinder blocks and pulling from the weeds that had grown up through it. With the flip of a few corroded levers on the dash-panel, the lumbering truck thrust forward, dragging a mangled skirt of weeds clinging to its rear.

Eloi zipped up alongside the two rangers, his eyes bright. "She's useful!" He nodded toward Betty.

"My uncle had a classic hover-car." Betty shrugged. "Not quite as old as this, but he would always let me help him work on it."

Eloi patted the dash lovingly. "I knew she'd still run. She just needed a little sweet-talkin', that's all. They don't make 'em like this anymore," he said with a grin. "Now what are ya waitin' for? Get in. Let's go."

Betty tugged on the passenger door handle. The hinges creaked loudly, then the door fell to the ground at her feet.

Eloi leaned over and looked out. "Oh, I've been meanin' to fix that."

The two rangers climbed into the cab, and the old truck sped off across the desert. Occasionally, the craft would jog slightly as it encountered a dip or slight rise and then return to its smooth passage as its pilot compensated for the change in terrain. A swirling trail of dust pursued the rickety old rusty heap as it weaved its way between cactus and prickly shrubs in a slalom motion, carrying the two rangers and their new guide swiftly in the direction of Shangri-la, nestled high in the mountain range to the west of Metropolis.

It was late afternoon when the change in sound of Eloi decelerating the droning engine of the hover-truck woke Betty from a deep sleep. She opened her eyes and noticed her head resting on Jett's shoulder as a pillow. She sat up straight. A little embarrassed, she said, apologetically, "So sorry. I didn't mean to ..."

"It's O.K.," said Jett. "I wish I could've slept that good."

"Welcome to Shangri-la." Eloi turned down a side street that headed for the ship yards.

The economy of Shangri-la revolved around the interplanetary ship building industry. The majority of structures consisted of manufacturing plants, hangars, launching pads and loading docks. The rest were subdivision housing and a few market squares.

Eloi pulled off the road next to a produce stand and stopped. "I have to get something before we leave," he said, exiting the truck.

The two rangers watched from inside the cab as he bought three coconuts from the vendor and placed them inside a burlap bag that he had brought with him.

When he climbed back into the cab with the coconuts, Betty asked, "What are those for?"

"Bargaining chips," he said with a wink and a grin as he stepped on the accelerator.

At the edge of the city, they took a small gravel road to the right that ran along a narrow ledge, hugging a steep, rocky cliff that jutted upward, shading the road as it curved around the bend. Betty peered over Jett's lap through the opening of the missing door. The ledge at the edge of the road was a sheer drop, straight down. She couldn't tell how far down because the clouds had crept up to the edge of the mountain, shrouding the rocky foothills far below in rolling blankets of mist. The same sensation began rising within her that she felt when they almost went over the ledge in Jett's car the day before. She wondered to herself if she was becoming prone to vertigo.

As the rusty old truck rounded the corner, the road opened up to a wide, flat shelf, a ledge apparently carved out of the rock. The facility had one main building that hung halfway over the edge, supported by slanting struts below. The yard was a seemingly disorganized maze of discarded parts that resembled a scrapyard more than anything else. From above, it would appear as a giant eagle's nest of metal, perched on the side of the cliff, perfectly secluded from the rest of the city.

Eloi brought the truck to a stop near a large open hangar bay door. Turning to Jett and Betty before exiting the truck, he said, "Stay out here for now. And let me do all the talking."

A faded sign of peeling paint hung above the door: *Skippy's Rocket Repair.* The two rangers stood by the doorway, waiting just outside.

A man who appeared to be in his late sixties, wearing a welder's cap, came out of the office to meet Eloi.

"Eloi Lightfoot? I t'ought you was gone dead!"

With a nod of his head and a slight smirk, Eloi responded, "Well, it's good to see you, too, Skipper." They shook hands and patted each other on the shoulder, like old friends.

As the two walked back toward the office, the skipper put his arm on Eloi's shoulder. "Well, Mr. Lightfoot, what can I did for you t'day?"

The sound of turbine testing machines made the outer walls of the building vibrate from their low hum. Metallic banging and the smell of oil and burning electricity filled the air as the skipper's employees went about their work. Eloi and the skipper could be seen negotiating through half-open blinds of the office window.

Jett and Betty walked along the side of the building to the edge of the cliff and gazed out over the expanse. Two hawks were gliding through the air, just below, riding the thermal currents that swooped up along the steep rise of the mountain. The two birds appeared to be engaged in a graceful aerial ballet. A violent gust of wind whipped at the rangers, strong enough to push them over if they had been standing too close to the edge.

"Ooh!" said Betty, catching herself. "This may not be a safe place to stand." She took a few steps back.

"Beauty and danger many times seem to go hand in hand," said Jett.

Betty couldn't help but smile a little, then realized he was referring to the hawks.

"Do you ever wish you could fly?" she asked.

"Right now would be a great time to fly," said Jett. "Then I could stay off this sprained ankle."

They both chuckled.

"Might I ask you a personal question?" asked Betty.

Jett looked a bit nervous but hesitantly said, "You might."

"After hearing of all your accomplishments as a field ranger—and they are admirable, I might add—I never knew that you were one so prone to being separated from his gun, until our meeting with the director the other day ..."

Jett frowned. "Your question?"

"How does one get into all the crazy situations you find yourself in, lose his gun, and still stay alive as long as you have?"

Jett's frown lines became noticeably deeper. "Well, first of all, I wouldn't say *lose*. That's an improper word for this context."

"I certainly don't mean any disrespect by it," Betty assured him. "I just mean, how do you recover from that so many times?"

"*Losing* is what you did back there on the road," he said, raising his voice.

"Oh, sorry. You're pretty sensitive about this, aren't you? And about that road thing, you're the one who couldn't avoid hitting a pothole the size of Bootleg Canyon."

His jaw stiffened a little, "I'm not ... *sensitive* ... about it. It's just that you're oversimplifying. That's all. Besides, losing your gun doesn't mean losing your weapon, it only means losing your gun."

She laughed, then abruptly caught herself. "I really am sorry."

He was now quite agitated, and Betty found a strange sense of humorous satisfaction from it.

"What I mean is," he continued, "the most effective weapon there is, you always have with you—your mind. As long as you keep a cool mind and don't panic, you'll always—"

Betty found herself laughing again, then quickly covered her mouth with her hand.

"*What?*"

"Sorry, I didn't mean to. It's just ... that answer is straight out of the Ranger Corps Handbook ... almost verbatim."

"Then you should know it already and not have to ask

these silly—"

At that moment, Eloi came walking through the doorway. "Come on, you two. We're ready to go." He waved his arm.

Jett wasted no time heading back to the hangar. Betty casually followed behind, a slight bounce in her step and a growing smirk.

A rocket ship was being moved into the launch bay—a bulky, decommissioned, military lunar cruiser that once was an orbit patrol ship in the days when Earth used the moon as a military base. The ship resembled a giant elongated bullet, with a needle-point hornet's nose protruding from the front like a jouster's lance, housing the antennas for deep-space transmission and reception. Its cylindrical body tapered in diameter to the atomic propulsion thrusters, jutting at the rear, just behind three small stabilizer wings. The hull was mustard yellow, with a starburst of red paint and gold trim that splashed the nose and streaked to the center of the main bulkhead, which had three small porthole windows on each side. When the ship came to a stop, an oval-shaped door on the side of the fuselage opened, and an iron stepladder extended down to the floor. Above the door, displayed in careful, hand-painted lettering, read the ship's name, *Ares*. Perched for take-off, the ship was facing a hangar bay door that was now retracting, revealing cloudy sky on the cliff drop-off side of the hangar.

They entered the cruiser, and the whole hangar began to hum as the ship's reactors powered up. The skipper and his crew of one were already on board, prepping the ship for take-off. When the ladder retracted and the door closed, the skipper, sitting at the head of the cabin with his first mate, turned to his passengers. "Everyone done got seat and buckle down; we're ready for blast."

When the hangar door had fully opened, a high-pitched whine emanated from the ship, and with a thruster blast that roared with the sound of Niagara Falls, they rocketed through the opening and immediately curved upward, quickly piercing through a layer of high cirrus clouds.

Betty looked out of the small porthole to her left and watched the features of the mountains below lose their detail. As they broke the atmosphere, she heard Gus, the first mate, say to the skipper, "Alright, next stop, Aurora Four."

She turned to Jett, who had taken out his grandfather's pistol and was thoughtfully examining it.

"I sure hope you know what you're doing," she said.

He quickly glanced at her and reholstered the pistol. Funny, he thought, he had been thinking the same thing about Eloi.

Betty settled into her seat and glanced at Jett. He wore a glum expression. The ship banked a hard right. A bright gray splash of craters instantly filled the windows from across the cabin as they swiftly dashed by the moon. The *Ares* yawed slightly as she shook herself clear of the moon's gravity, then leaped smoothly into free space. Thrusters were raised to full cruise as the ship straightened its course through the empty vacuum and shot off in the direction of the Orion constellation.

CHAPTER FIVE

THE VALUE OF COCONUTS

It was quiet inside the cabin of the *Ares*, except for the slight hum of the main thrusters from the rear and the occasional sip of coffee taken by the skipper as he monitored the gauges up front.

Captain Rogers slowly opened his eyes. It was his first full night's rest in three days. The small of his back felt stiff, and his shoulder was numb. Even though the chairs reclined, they were not the most comfortable for sleeping. As he stretched and sat up, he noticed that he had been resting his head on Betty's shoulder as she slept in the chair next to him. He rubbed his face, and his hand felt wet. *Drool.* He glanced at Betty.

"Oh, great," he whispered. Betty's sleeve was wet. Leaning over, Jett tried to wipe it off with his own sleeve, trying not to wake her.

"Well, goot mornin', Cap'n Rogers," came a boisterous greeting from the skipper, spinning his chair.

"Shh," Jett jerked his head toward the skipper and nervously pleaded with his eyes as he wiped at Betty's sleeve.

She opened her eyes, blinking. "W-what are you doing?" she said sleepily.

Jett straightened and slowly moved away, hoping she wouldn't notice.

She inspected her sleeve. "What did you do?"

Jett opened his mouth to speak, but no words came. He couldn't think of anything to say without incriminating himself. He decided the best approach was just to ignore it.

Jett moved to the front and placed his hand on the skipper's shoulder. "How close are we?"

"Perfect timin', Cap'n Rogers," replied the skipper. "I was gett'n ready to wake everyone." He reached to the control panel and pushed a lever up, locking it into the off position, causing the main thrusters to whine down, then disengage.

Betty began wiping her sleeve on her pants, a puzzled look on her face.

The planet Neptune loomed large in the ship's starboard side windows, a glowing sphere of swirling shades of blue. Above its atmosphere, in the empty vacuum of high orbit, darted small specks, hundreds of foreign spaceships, crisscrossing paths in the iridescent distance.

"There she is. The roulette city, Aurora Four." Gus pointed at the space to the lower left of Neptune.

Betty walked up to the front of the cabin, stood beside Jett and peered out, scanning the lower horizon, straining to find the point Gus had indicated. "Are you talking about that small moon over there?" she pointed.

"That's no moon," came the voice of Eloi from behind. "Aurora Four is an abandoned orbital point station that was used back when Neptune was a more successful mining planet. But now, because of its mostly desolate and extreme remote location, it's become a thriving center for illegal gambling, speakeasys, and whatever other illicit activities you can imagine."

"A haven for criminals of all kinds—a rat's nest," interjected Jett.

Eloi nodded. "We must use extreme caution."

———

As the *Ares* drew near, the station's structural attributes became more visible. It looked like a giant donut-wheel of glass and metal, slowly spinning in Neptune's faint outer glow. The wheel spun perpendicular to the planet's surface, its centrifugal force acting as a primitive form of artificial gravity.

The outermost portion of the wheel was dark and metallic, dotted with pin hole lights from the occasional window, while the innermost portion of the wheel was ablaze with the twinkling glow of multicolored neon signage, which shone through the glass-covered domed roof of the inner wheel that circled around on itself. It was this neon glow that emanated from the satellite's center, producing an ever-pulsating iridescent aurora, that earned the old space station its adopted name, Aurora Four.

To access the station, ships docked at the mooring pier—a large docking station that traveled in synchronized orbit just off from Aurora Four. Cargo and passengers would then be shuttled between the two.

As soon as Gus had maneuvered the ship into position, locking the *Ares* airtight to her assigned docking port, Eloi motioned to him and the skipper. "Watch the ship till we get back."

"You'll got no argue from me," said the skipper, chuckling and shaking his head.

The first mate turned to the skipper. "Say, Skipps. Since we're all the way out here anyway, it won't hurt for me to just go walking around a little."

The skipper frowned at him. "Better you no go, Gus. You know how you are aroun' place like dis."

Before exiting the hatch behind Jett and Betty, Eloi turned back to the two still inside. "We don't plan to be long. Keep the engines warm."

Gus plopped back down in his chair and wrinkled his nose. "Nuts!"

The two rangers and Eloi boarded a shuttle and crossed over to the satellite.

———

Emerging from the shuttle's arrivals lobby, the three entered the main square of the station's inner surface, under the enormous clear-tube ceiling.

Eloi scanned the area. "If I know Melvin, if he's here, he's in one of three places. Come on, this way."

"If he's here?" snapped Jett. "You mean it's possible we came all the way out here for nothing?"

"It's been a long time," replied Eloi. "But look, you've always got to start somewhere. Melvin is a creature of old habits, and old habits are hard to break."

Jett and Betty exchanged glances. Jett hoped that he would not have to admit he was wrong about putting his trust in the old man. Neither did he want to hear the words *I told you so* from Betty.

They gained attention from many unwelcoming eyes of shady individuals passing by as they ventured down a dark and dirty alleyway. After all, much of Aurora Four's appeal to those who frequented it was the lack of Space Ranger presence. The rhythmic clamor of various alien renditions of jazz, blues, and swing belched from open doors, spilling into the alleyway and mingling in the artificial atmosphere above in a kaleidoscope of sound. The satellite was a haven for revelry, where old vices of debauchery flourished most strongly.

Betty peered into the distance of the constant, upward-sloping terrain of neon-smothered bars, nightclubs, and casinos. She followed the clustered curve of buildings with her eyes through the clear tubing above as it swooped upward, then overhead and back around, completing the circuit behind them. She stepped on a crack in the walkway and lost her balance, falling back into Jett. "Sorry," she said, faintly embarrassed. "It's just, this place ... it's a lot to take in. It's much larger than I thought it would be. I've heard of it but never been here before."

"Not many have," replied Jett, helping her to an upright position again. "It attracts only a certain crowd."

After checking two casinos that failed to produce Eloi's contact, with Eloi leading the way, the three proceeded down an eerily dark dead-end corridor. A bright sign at the end, atop a dimly lit three-story night club, flashed red letters in sequential order: *Mickey's*.

Eloi halted the two rangers outside. "Remember, let me do all the talking. He gets a little skittish around strangers, but I know how to make him sing."

Mickey's nightclub was packed, as it was most nights. It was the epicenter of the solar system's underbelly, a favorite dive for those who traveled in shadier circles. The main room was a mostly circular auditorium, congested with a plethora of tables of varying sizes. Curtain-shrouded private booths discreetly lined the side walls. The room was filled with a heavy smoke that gathered at the ceiling, swirling and churning, like an ominous, looming thunderstorm, highlighted by incandescent upward-beaming embedded table lamps below.

Bathed in the wash of an imperial blue spotlight, a Venusian vixen with reptilian features seductively crooned a very bluesy rendition of "Fever." Just behind her, a small band coolly kept the hypnotic, slow beat on the main stage, front and center.

Once inside, Eloi motioned the two rangers with a subtle nod of his head. "He usually sits in that booth over there in the corner. You two go around that way, and we'll approach from either side."

He glanced quickly across the room. "Be careful."

Jett and Betty each responded with a nod of their own and set off around the left edge of the room.

When Eloi turned back, his path was blocked by a big black robot that stood immediately in front of him, lights blinking and gears turning under its glass-domed head. Round antennas whirred on the side where a man's ears would be. It had a deep, monotone, simulated-human voice. "Drink, sir?"

Eloi lowered his eyes to the drinks on the tray, at the end of the robot's bulbous arm. He stared at them and swallowed hard. He was drunk when the two rangers found him the other night, and it embarrassed him. He didn't consider himself a drunkard but would make himself numb to old memories from time to time. But tonight, he felt alive again. He was on a ranger mission, and he would not mess that up.

A voice shouted from three tables over, "Hey, Robby, over here! Three more!"

The robot turned and left Eloi standing alone, his arm still rising unconsciously to grasp the glass that was no longer there. The old man sighed and looked down at his empty hand. His heart was pounding. "That was close," he whispered.

The presence of rangers in the nightclub was not enough to make a scene. But enough heads in the joint turned to look their way that it caught Melvin's attention—a small, green Martian, sitting in a side booth by himself in the corner. When Melvin realized that the two rangers were making their way toward him, he darted out the booth to flee in the opposite direction and ran smack into the knees of Eloi, who was waiting just to the side.

The Martian's high-pitched voice barely cut through the music throbbing in the background. "Oh, no! It wasn't the airplanes. It was Beauty killed the beast! Pay no attention to that man behind the curtain! Mother of mercy, is this the end of Rico?"

Eloi lifted the aging Martian up under the shoulders, like a small child, and plopped him back down in the booth. "Take it easy, Melvin. I'm not here to arrest you ... this time." Eloi sat down next to him.

Melvin rapidly blinked his beady eyes, then leaned forward to get a closer look. "Eloi Lightfoot? I thought you were dead. Thought you a goner. Ya know, like ..." He slid his finger across his throat and made a vulgar sound with his tongue.

The ex-ranger gazed down at him. His long white hair seemed to glow phosphorescently from the neon-blue backlit room just outside the booth. "I'm just an old ghost," he responded, "returning to one of his familiar haunts."

Melvin pulled his glass closer to him, the one he had been nursing before he spotted the rangers, his feet dangling from the seat. He spoke very fast and bumped Eloi on the shoulder with the side of a closed fist. "Whaddya hear? Whaddya say?" The Martian's voice sounded almost comical, as if he had sucked on a helium balloon.

Eloi directed Melvin's attention with a glance. "These are some friends of mine, Jett and Betty." The two rangers slid into the seat opposite the table. "We seem to have a riddle that requires your expertise."

Jett and Betty both reached across the table to shake hands with the Martian, and each uttered a polite greeting.

The Martian glanced at Jett, wrinkled his face, and grunted. But when he saw Betty, his tiny eyes opened big and twinkled. Two antennae wiggled atop his head. "Of all the gin joints in all the towns in all the world, she walks into mine." He reached over, grabbed her hand, and started licking it.

"Stop that! Gross!" She recoiled her arm.

Melvin just sat staring at her with an open-mouthed, one-tooth grin, eyes squinting. "Hee hee hee hee hee hee hee."

She was so disgusted, she couldn't help but respond, "You're just a slimy little toad, aren't you!"

Jett put his hand on her wrist. "*Betty* ...!" he whispered.

Melvin shrugged. "I'm no good at being noble, but it doesn't take much to see that the problems of three little people don't amount to a hill of beans in this crazy world. Someday you'll understand that. Now, now ... Here's looking at you kid." He raised his glass to her and drank.

Betty stared, puzzled.

Eloi frowned. "He learned American English from the cinema. He can hardly speak the language without quoting old movies."

Melvin licked his hand and slicked his antennae back, eyes locked on Betty. "You need to be kissed. And often. And by someone who knows how!"

"Melvin!" said Eloi sharply. "What can you tell us about this?" He nodded at Jett, who produced the circuit panel from his pocket.

The Martian took the panel, gave it a quick look, then gasped, speaking very fast. "Where did you find this? You know what happens to nosey fellows?"

"What do you know about it?" asked Eloi.

"Um ..." The Martian began to stutter. "N-nope"

Eloi's expression grew dark. "You've never been a very good liar, Melvin. Come now, tell us where this came from."

Melvin stared helplessly at Eloi for a few moments. Little beads of sweat began to form on the purple freckles of his forehead. "Who knows what evil lurks in the hearts of men?" He forced a hard swallow. "The Shadow knows."

Eloi sighed. "Alright, Melvin, let's cut to the chase and get right down to it." He reached into his bag and pulled out one coconut.

Melvin froze, his antennae erect. Eloi placed it on the table in front of him and started gently rolling it in small circles with his index finger. "Surely, you're starting to remember now. Aren't you, Melvin?"

The Martian's eyes were fixed on the spinning coconut, almost hypnotized by it. He sat on his hands and began bouncing in the seat, like a small child trying to hold his bladder. The beads of sweat became more pronounced, and he began licking his chops.

His breathing became a heavy panting that steadily increased until finally he broke. "Give it!"

In a flash, he snatched the coconut and held it firmly to his chest, cradling it with both arms. He gently brought it up to his cheek and began stroking it, as you would a pet cat. Rocking back and forth, he began humming quietly, happily to himself.

Betty leaned over to Jett, her hand cupping her mouth. "I never knew Martians were such eccentric critters."

Jett muttered under his breath, "I've never seen one react this way either."

"Eloi sure picked a doozy of an informant." She sat back and folded her arms.

When it comes to the delicate art of interrogating Martians, the two rangers were beginning to realize the value of coconuts.

"O.K., Melvin, you know the drill," said Eloi. "To keep the coconut, you know what I need from you."

The Martian's face went sour. He whimpered like a puppy, then stood in his seat and raised a finger. "Do not speak to me of rules. This is war! This is not a game of cricket!"

"Then I'll be needing my coconut back," said Eloi dryly.

The Martian snitch gripped the coconut even tighter in his arms and plopped back down in his seat, continuing to rub his cheek against it, his lower lip fighting a quiver.

Eloi sighed and looked across the table at the two rangers. "This may take a while."

Betty moved to rise from the table and put her hand on Jett's shoulder. "This is all very fascinating, but if you'll please excuse me, I need to go, um ... powder my nose."

"Sure." Jett slid over to let her out, then sat back down. He watched her make her way across the room. When she reached the parlor, she quickly glanced back and disappeared to the right.

This was very curious to Jett, because when he had passed by that room earlier, he noticed the restrooms were to the left. The opening to the right only led to a visi-phone booth. What was she up to? Who would she be calling from out here?

Eloi continued interrogating the Martian, more sternly now than before. "Melvin! Tell me what you know about this board."

The Martian, aside from his antics, looked up at him with a seemingly genuine, dreadful fear.

Eloi turned to his bag again. "Very impressive, Melvin. I see you have stronger willpower now than you used to. What does this do for you?" He placed the second coconut on the table.

Melvin's beady eyes seemed to bulge. He got really quiet and still. "You brought two? You dirty rat! Nothing's too good for the man who shot Liberty Valance." His mouth opened and he started licking his lips and rubbing his fingers together. Jett could tell by the expression on his face that his mind was working hard. He was trying to think of something he could offer Eloi that would allow him to keep the two coconuts. "What if I just give you ... a name? The, uh, stuff that dreams are made of. Even trade?" he said, softly.

"That would be a very good start."

Melvin's face went very serious. "This is just between us, right? You and me. No one else. Maybe him." He glanced at Jett then back to Eloi. "You make promise?"

Eloi put his elbows on the table and leaned over toward the Martian. "In all of our experiences, have I ever let you down?"

An angry frown twisted Melvin's face. "Ranger's promise. Do it!"

"O.K., Melvin, if you wish."

Melvin scowled at him, waiting. "We didn't need dialogue, we had faces. Now say it!"

Of course, there was no such thing as a *ranger's promise*. A ranger's word was as good as gold. But somehow, saying it this way seemed to make all the difference to the Martian, so Eloi humored him.

"Alright, ranger's promise."

Melvin stood up on the seat, leaned over Eloi's shoulder, cupped his hand to his mouth, and whispered a name that sent shivers down his spine, just from saying it.

Eloi brought his hand to his chin and pondered what the Martian had said for a moment. "Hmm ... Rog. Are you sure?"

For a split second, the Martian went nuts, then spasmodically shushed Eloi. "That's a name you don't say aloud around parts like these, you knuckle-head! Do you want to wake up with a Snurku head in your bed? The syndicate has eyes and ears everywhere." He put his hand up in front of Eloi's mouth and quickly looked all around nervously. He then clutched his hand to his mouth, realizing that he had given away more than he intended. "Well, here's another nice mess you've gotten me into! If word got out that I gave you information like this, I'd be a dead Martian walking. Sleeping with the fishes. Drifting with the meteors."

Jett squinted curiously at Eloi. "The Martian syndicate?

Eloi nodded grimly. "I was afraid of this. I just needed a reliable source to confirm it."

It was about this time that Betty returned. "I'm back. Did I miss anything?"

Jett stood once more to let her in and observed her suspiciously as she slid to the inside of the booth.

"Melvin," Eloi said softly, "where can we find him?"

Melvin clutched at Eloi's sleeve and tugged on it. "Please, no more questions. All I can say. I'm melting, mel-l-lting ..."

"I have to know, Melvin."

"I can't, I can't."

Eloi placed the third coconut on the table with the second. "How about now?"

"Three?" Melvin began breathing heavy, tightly clutching the first coconut in his arms. "And in the end, you wind up dyin' all alone on some dusty street. For what? For a tin star. It's all for nothin'. It's all for nothin'." He forced himself to look away and stared straight at the wall beside him. "I need money more than coconuts. I'm stranded. Can't win. It's a cruel satellite. I coulda had class. I coulda been a contender. I coulda been somebody, instead of a bum, which is what I am, let's face it." He turned to face Eloi again. "I'd like to see Mars one last time before the big croak." His voice broke, and he began sobbing.

He looked pathetic and pitiful, sunken in his seat, holding the coconut up over his face to hide his tears.

"There's no place like home! There's no place like home!"

Jett cast a doubtful glance toward Eloi. An unsympathetic frown distorted the old man's features. The savvy ex-ranger was familiar with this Martian's antics and was not fooled by his dramatic distractions.

Eloi leaned over and said in the Martian's ear, "The planet Mars is on our agenda, if you're interested."

The Martian froze. "I'm listening."

"You tell us where we can find Ro ... uh, this fella you mentioned, and I think we can arrange to give you a lift." Eloi glanced at Jett and winked.

Like a frog snatching a fly from the air, in a flash, the Martian snatched the two remaining coconuts to his chest. "We all go a little mad sometimes." He fumbled with the coconuts, trying to keep all three close. "I think this is the beginning of a beautiful friendship."

When the rangers arrived back at the *Ares*, the skipper was asleep in his chair with his feet propped up on the forward instrument panel. He abruptly awoke and nearly fell from his perch when Betty banged on the hatch for him to let them in. Gus was gone.

"Where's your first mate?" asked Jett.

"Dat hard-headed beef-wit just had ta go out. Dare wus no stopping 'im."

Jett sighed, looking at Eloi. "Great."

"Well, we do have a little time to kill," said Eloi. "We've got an extra passenger we're taking with us to Mars. He'll meet us here shortly. He had to grab a few of his personal things. Plus, he didn't want to be seen leaving the bar with rangers."

"After he got what he wanted, don't you think he'll just split and never show?" said Betty. "Can you really trust this senile old Martian, Eloi?"

"Martian?" the skipper erupted. "You no bringin' no dirty garten slug on my ship! Are you crazy-nuts?" He gestured violently, twirling his hands in the air. He paced the floor back and forth, his face red with anger. "You probably even give it coconut!"

"I don't think you have to worry, Skipper," said Betty. "I seriously doubt that shifty creature will even show."

The skipper turned and scowled back at Eloi. "For his sake, I hope not. 'Cause he will not ride! Not on my ship! How can you did this ta me, Eloi?" He turned to the front, still mumbling to himself.

Two knocks clanked faintly from outside the hatch. Eloi stepped over and, looking down through the porthole, said, "Ah, here's our little green friend now."

"Well, whadda ya know." Betty was thoroughly impressed.

"No! Don't let it in!" said the skipper, as Eloi opened the hatch and invited the Martian aboard.

"Whaddya hear? Whaddya say?" said Melvin casually.

"Get it! Eject! Out wid you!" The skipper gritted his teeth and, with both fists clenched, marched forcefully toward Eloi. "What I tell you? Get it off!"

Melvin quickly dropped his bag and ducked behind Eloi, hiding behind his legs. "Danger, Will Robinson!" His voice sounded even higher than it did in the club.

Eloi put his hands up. "Skipper, just calm down. It'll be O.K. Trust me."

"Trust you? Da last time I trust you wid' Martian, I had ta scrub da whole ship ..."

There came a sudden violent pounding on the door from outside. It was Gus. They couldn't hear anything through the airtight glass, but the expression on his face and silent mouthing of his lips seemed to be saying, "Let me in!" He frantically glanced behind him.

Jett reached over and unlatched the door, opening it. "What's wrong?"

Gus leaped inside and stumbled to the floor. He was breathing heavily; sweat dripped from his face, and his shirt was torn. "Close it! Close it quick! We gotta go now!" He got up quickly and started for the control panel.

"What's going on?" asked Betty.

Jett stooped and looked through the porthole. "Would it have something to do with the three angry-looking chaps exiting that last shuttle?"

Gus plopped down in the pilot's chair. "Yes, it would, but it's all just a big misunderstanding, that's all," he said, as the engines roared, throttling up.

The skipper walked up to Gus and grabbed him by the shoulder. "We can't leave yet, you nincompoop! We gotta git dis ting off!" He nodded with his head.

"What are you so ruffled about, old man?"

The skipper just stood fuming at Gus with a fistful of torn shirt in his hand. Gus looked back at the two rangers and Eloi. They all glanced back at Melvin, huddled in the corner, holding his bag of stuff, grinning big.

"Oh, I see," said Gus.

Gus' pursuers were running across the platform toward the ship, ray guns drawn. They fired on the *Ares*.

"What?" exclaimed the skipper, turning.

"That's what I've been trying to tell you!" shouted Gus.

"Go! Go!" The skipper started flailing his arms and slapped Gus on the back of the head.

The ship snapped away from its docking and thrust forward, sending everyone not seated to the floor.

The *Ares* swiftly curved upward to the right, leaving Neptune's orbit and Aurora Four as a distant speck to stern. The skipper climbed into his chair next to Gus. "O.K., spill it. What happen back dere?"

Gus looked at him, shrugging. "I told you, it was just a misunderstanding. That's all."

The skipper stared him down sternly. "Yeah, what I say. Is always misunderstand wit' you. You should never gone out." He turned and glared at Melvin, who returned an awkward forced grin. Then he scowled at Eloi and shook his head.

––––––––

After the ship had been cruising in open space for a few hours and half the passengers began to doze off, Melvin scooted up to Betty, raised his eyebrows twice, and tilted his chin up, trying to appear suave and sophisticated, the way he had seen it done in so many Earth picture shows. "What is it you want, Mary? What do you want? You want the moon? Just say the word, and I'll throw a lasso around it and pull it down."

"Get your hand off my leg, please." Betty shoved it away. "I don't like your manners."

"I'm not crazy about yours. I didn't ask to see you. I don't mind if you don't like my manners. I don't like them myself. They're pretty bad. I grieve over them long winter evenings." The Humphrey Bogart line didn't sound right at all, coming from the Martian.

"Stop it!" she swiped his hands away again.

"Emily, I have a little confession to make. I really am a horse doctor, but marry me and I'll never look at any other horse."

Most everyone in the cabin didn't pay much attention to what was going on. The Martian was harassing her, but Betty was a ranger, and rangers were quite capable of taking care of themselves.

Jett was watching out of the corner of his eye, pretending to be half asleep, curious to see how much Betty would take until she finally did something about it.

"Look, you little weasel!" She was quite angry now. "I'm not kidding. If you don't keep your hands off me, you're going to get it!"

"Why don't you come up sometime 'n' see me?" The Martian's antennae wiggled. Melvin started pointing back and forth. "Jane. Tarzan. Jane. Tarzan. C'mon, who's your favorite Martian?" He ran his hand down the small of her back.

"That's *it*!"

"Ooh! Weeoo weeoo!" The Martian's face was flat against the floor, grimacing in pain. "S-t-e-l-l-a!"

Betty stood over him, locking his arm in a twisting wrist-hold. "Alright, you little lech. Are you going to behave, or do I have to remove your arm from its socket?"

The Martian squirmed on the floor but couldn't free himself. Every time he tried to move, Betty would apply a little more pressure to the wrist and elbow. Everyone was watching. Jett was quietly laughing.

"Ooh weeoo! Sorry, baby! I'm sorry! Ugh!"

"It's Betty!" She grunted and pushed harder.

"Ooh weeoo! Sorry, baby! Betty! Betty, I'm sorry! You're tearing me apart!"

Jett stopped laughing. His face went sour. "What's that smell?"

Betty let go of the Martian and stepped away, covering her nose with her hand. "Oh! What is tha—"
Her eyes bulged, and she suppressed a gag.

Eloi turned around in his chair and sighed, "Oh, no."

Melvin got to his feet. "Round up the usual suspects."

The skipper jumped to his feet and pointed at Eloi, enraged. "I knew it! I knew it! You give it coconut! You stupit ..." The skipper then went to his knees, choking.

By this time, everyone in the cabin had their nose buried in their shirt sleeve or handkerchief, trying to mask the odor, except for Melvin. He was backing into the corner with a very guilty look on his face. "Sorry, fellas; it's not my fault." He pointed at Betty. "She made me do it."

She glared back at him with a look that could pierce through steel.

Melvin quickly crossed his arms and innocently looked the other way. "Insanity runs in my family. It practically gallops."

The smell permeated every cranny of the ship like a noxious swamp vapor. Betty now knew why none of the establishments on the satellite carried coconuts for the Martians; it was obviously too much of a liability.

The skipper got up and marched very indignantly toward

Melvin. "You stinkin', slimy, green-bellied space-rat! I jettison you!"

The Martian's eyes went big. He sank to the floor, then scurried to the other side of the cabin. "Sanctuary! Sanctuary!"

"Wait!" Eloi stood and intercepted the skipper, throwing his arms around him. "Calm down, old man. Let's not be brash."

"Brash? Brash!" The skipper trembled, he was so angry. "Dat ting you feed coconut soil our air! Mars long way trip!"

"It'll be alright," said Eloi. "We just won't let him have any more till we arrive."

"More?" The skipper was flummoxed, eyes bulging, mouth gaping. "You give it *more*? I really tink you losing it, old man." The skipper stepped away from Eloi and crossed his arms. "O.K., Martian can stay. But it ride in back, in cargo hold."

Melvin looked at Eloi sympathetically.

Eloi sighed. "You better do it, Melvin. You've blown your privileges."

"In more ways than one," came Betty's muffled voice through her shirt. She was holding her nose too.

Melvin's shoulders sank, his face pouting. He made his way through the door to the cargo hold, dragging his bag behind him.

"No!" The skipper took off. "Coconut stay here!"

Melvin turned to see the skipper bounding through the door after him and scurried like a weasel to the back of the compartment.

Everyone in the cabin up front could hear Melvin through the hatch opening. "Madness. Madness!"

"Hand over dat bag, you slimy little ... oop!"

"Spread out!"

A ruckus of jostling and smacking ensued in the cargo hold.

"Give over!"

"Shove off! Weeoo!"

It went quiet for a few seconds, and then the skipper finally emerged from the room, dragging the bag behind him and sporting what looked like it might become a black eye. He threw the bag to the floor in the corner and looked at Eloi, who was smirking.

"Shut up," snapped the skipper as he marched past Eloi. "Dis will cost more on bill, ya know."

Eloi smiled and said under his breath, "I'm sure the rangers are good for it."

A tiny, muffled voice could be heard from behind the locked door of the cargo hold. "You think I'm licked. You all think I'm licked. Well, I'm not licked. And I'm going to stay right here and fight for this lost cause. Even if this room gets filled with lies like these, and the Taylors and all their armies come marching into this place."

The skipper eased into his chair and glanced at Gus, who was smirking also. "Oh, shut up, smiley-mouth. Dis all your fault too!"

CHAPTER SIX

ANGRY RED PLANET

Captain Jethro Rogers sat staring out the view-port of the *Ares*, unconsciously fingering the grip of his grandfather's holstered pistol. The red glow of Mars blazed through the window. The skipper had settled the *Ares* into a high-orbit shipping lane, miles above the planet's surface.

Melvin was up front directing Eloi where to go; then Eloi would relay the information to the skipper because the skipper was now refusing to speak to the Martian or even acknowledge his presence on board.

As the ship descended through the outer atmosphere, the barren features of the scorched planet reflected in the circular glass window before Jett.

The *Ares* made one half revolution past the dark side of the planet, when Melvin stood up and pointed. "There," he said, in a high-pitched tone. "Set down there. We're not in Kansas anymore."

The skipper checked his map. "Dat's no place to land! It's eleven mile from port!"

Eloi put his hand on the skipper's shoulder. "I think in our case, old friend, it would be better if we grounded out here away from things, where our landing will go less noticed."

"Hmm. O.K., friend," said the skipper, "but the walk's all you."

Betty looked at Jett and sighed, remembering their trek to Eloi's house a few nights before.

"How about that crater over there, Skipps?" asked Gus. "We can hide the ship in that crop of wild mushrooms."

"Yes, dat's goot place," replied the skipper.

Jett had been casually listening to the conversation up front as he stared out the window, until it finally dawned on him. "Eleven miles? Oh, great."

"It looks like you'll only have to walk about three of those," said Gus. "There appears to be a transit post along that road about two miles west of the crater."

Jett strode to the head of the cabin and peered out. Before the ship descended past the rim of the giant crater, he saw the mono-lane dirt trail Gus had indicated, which disappeared in the direction of another great crater, way off in the distance across the barren red plain. Jett returned to secure his seat for landing and mumbled to himself sarcastically, "Well, today's our lucky day."

About that time, the skipper called out, "Everyone take seat, and prepare for stop!"

The retro-rockets kicked in below the ship with a rush of roaring hisses, gently nestling the *Ares* within a grand forest of wild Martian mushrooms. With a slight jolt, the ship came to rest in a small dale near the center of the crater.

When the dust had settled around the ship, Betty gazed through a porthole. "Wow, they're even more majestic than I imagined. The stereo-pictures I've seen don't begin to do them justice."

Eloi overheard her and responded, "Yes, the largest ones grow even taller than Earth's great sequoia trees. Besides minerals and ores, it's the most abundant resource Mars can produce."

Melvin went to the locker to retrieve his coconuts. "Try growing up as a Martian child eating only mushroom plap and mushroom flabber. Then see how majestic you think they are."

Betty peered back through the port. Dawn was just breaking over the rim of the crater. Ominous shafts of brilliant orange and crimson washed between the trunks of enormous mushrooms, towering far above the space ship. A shudder ran through her. The blood-red sky of the early Martian morning gave her an uneasy feeling of baneful ill-boding. They were in the heart of the Martian Sector—the same sector where three very experienced Space Rangers had been recently brutally assassinated. She shifted in her seat, glanced back at Eloi and Jett, and was reminded of her own extreme inexperience. In that moment though, she recognized an irony—three rangers, well, almost three, counting Eloi, investigating the deaths of three rangers. She wondered if their fates would be any different.

Eloi slipped into his poncho, stepped to the door, and turned. "Bring your ponchos. Mars is a little cooler than Earth. Plus, the two of you don't need to be walking around in the city with those uniforms showing so plainly. Humans are not particularly welcomed here, though they are tolerated."

"Probl'y 'cause most human peoples here be scoundrels back on Earth," interjected the skipper. "Smugglers, pirates an' such!"

"But rangers ..." Eloi paused for a moment. "Well, we won't be seeing any welcome mats."

Jett slipped into his poncho but stopped at the door. He wanted to ask Betty to stay on the ship with Gus and the skipper. It would be much safer for her here, and distractions would be limited between him and Eloi. He thought of his sprained ankle and how much help she had been for him, and he might need that again. The thought of asking Eloi for help with his walking troubled him more. He was conflicted. She had proven useful a few times already, but he was used to going it alone and used to following his instinct. He turned to Betty and said, "Betty, maybe you should ..."

"I'm coming with you." She said quickly, almost as if she anticipated what he was thinking.

He hesitated for a moment. "O.K., then." He put his hands up in resignation. "Let's go."

Eloi was already outside when the skipper remembered. "Oh yeah ..." He handed a small, palm-sized cylinder with a single button on it to Jett. "Use dis to let us know when ready for pickup. Jus make sure it not at *Grand Central,* if know what I mean."

"Thanks. Got it." said Jett.

The two rangers exited the ship.

Melvin was the last one to leave the cabin, and the skipper was pretending to pay him no attention, though he couldn't wait for him to vacate his ship.

The Martian, not yet feeling fully vindicated from the skipper's earlier treatment, turned to the front. "Here's one for the Gipper! Uh, Skipper ... enjoy!" He quickly scurried to the door, raised a leg and, quite audibly, flatulated one last time in the ship's cabin before slamming the door behind him. Melvin jumped to the ground and scampered from the ship as fast as he could, toting his bag of remaining coconuts over his shoulder and laughing maniacally, shouting, "It's alive! It's a-l-i-v-e!"

With a loud bang, the ship's hatch flew open, smacking against the hull. The skipper and Gus burst through the opening, tumbling over each other to the ground, coughing and wheezing.

"You stinkin' rat-skunk!" The skipper scrambled to get to his feet. "Good-for-nutt'n, lousy pig-dog!" He scooped a handful of stones and started throwing them wildly at the Martian.

The two rangers and Eloi ducked to get out of the way.

The skipper's face was red. He gritted his teeth and growled angrily. He was down to his last rock, and the Martian had almost reached cover at the edge of the mushroom forest, laughing increasingly louder with each failed attempt of the skipper's poor marksmanship. The skipper snorted and focused hard. Taking a deep breath and winding up like a pitcher on the mound, he released his final fast ball and hoped for a strike.

With a dull thud, the rock hit the Martian square on top of the head, just behind his left antenna.

A loud and agitated "Weeoo!" was heard, followed by profuse Martian cursing, just before Melvin disappeared into the clustered alien timberland.

Hands on her hips, Betty turned to Eloi and murmured, "I hope that wasn't supposed to be our guide."

Eloi calmly shook his head. "No. On the trek here I got all I needed out of him."

"Well, I got what I didn't need outa dat rat!" the skipper interjected. "No more for you!" He pointed at Eloi. "No more rats on my ship!"

Gus dusted off the gritty red dirt. "I agree, man. When those Martians depressurize, they can really split your sinuses."

Captain Rogers walked over to Eloi and stood next to him, staring in the direction Melvin had disappeared. "Well, show's over now; we need to hit the road."

Eloi nodded.

Even though it was about seven o'clock in the morning, Martian time, with the sun beginning to rise well in the sky, the path for the three rangers had become increasingly darker as they penetrated ever deeper into the mushroom forest. The ground of the crater bottom was moist, as it remained constantly shielded from the sun. Only once in a while would faint glints of sun rays flicker through the tightly packed umbrella-like canopy above. With every step, new-growth mushrooms squished under their feet, causing them to slip slightly now and then.

They had been walking for about an hour and still saw no sign of the outer edge of the thicket. Jett noticed that the longer they had walked, the quieter and more grim-faced Eloi had become.

"What's eatin' ya?" ventured Jett.

"I'm familiar with this 'Rog' fella," said Eloi. "He was nothin' but a chump back in my day, but was earning a growing reputation nonetheless. I wasn't really surprised to hear his name, though; his type is usually the kind to seize control of the syndicate. If they live long enough, that is."

"What's he like?" asked Betty.

Eloi pondered for a moment. "Basically, he clawed his way to the top with ruthless, blood-splattered efficiency. For example, even when animals fight each other, the loser communicates submissiveness by laying on their back and exposing their throat. In such situations, even the most hostile animal does not take advantage of the vanquished. Not this Rog fella, though. He'd kill you just the same as look at you, *especially* if he thought you were weak. Cowardice seems to excite a blood lust of some sort within him."

Eloi froze and remained silent.

"I heard it too," whispered Jett, straining to listen.

A muffled rustling in the distance swiftly grew to a small thunder. The clatter of hundreds of tiny scurrying feet amid a rolling noise of voracious squeals resonated increasingly louder between the mushrooms from the darkness around them.

"Myrtle-mice," groaned Eloi; his countenance sank. "Or rather, Vampire-rats."

Jett and Eloi drew their pistols.

"Keep moving, quickly!" said Eloi. "It's too late to be quiet; they already know we're here!"

Eloi ran with a frail, elderly gait. Jett resorted to hobbling along, trying to keep weight off of his sprained ankle. Betty was the only one capable of fully sprinting, and kept unintentionally bursting far ahead of the two men.

"Stick together!" Eloi shouted at her.

Betty halted and looked back. She stared, petrified by what she saw. The gigantic mushroom trunks around them began to vibrate. The darkest blackness in the distance began to envelop them on three sides from the rear, rolling and churning, like a fast-moving dark fog, as the faint outline of the Vampire-rats became clearer and clearer. She felt the ground slightly rumble beneath her feet. She gasped. "Oh, hurry! *Hurry!*"

Without stopping, Jett turned and fired a shot behind him. The flash of the laser bolt reflected thousands of pairs of red eyes, swarming violently toward them in the shadows. An agonizing squeal cut through the tumult as Jett's shot connected with one. It only seemed to invigorate the rest even more.

Jett's foot slipped on a squashed mushroom, and he immediately tumbled to the ground. Eloi grabbed his shirt by the shoulder. "Get up! Keep moving!"

Betty ran back toward Jett. "Get up! Come on!"

"Alright already!" said Jett, very agitated by all the orders. "I only slipped, that's all!"

Betty reached him and almost slid down herself when she tried to stop. She put her shoulder under his arm. "C'mon, I'll help you!"

"I'm alri ..." Jett didn't really need any help getting up, but he knew it was a waste of time to argue.

"O.K., sister, if you insist!" He turned and fired three more shots.

"I do insist. Now get moving!" she barked.

Eloi turned and started firing too. They all kept running. Every one of their shots had connected with a Vampire-rat. At this point, they were so close that it would have been impossible to miss hitting something. Flesh and fur started flying as the Vampire-rats swarmed around the fallen, and they cannibalized their own dead, growling and slashing in a hysterical frenzy. This halted some, but the rest continued to close in on the slow-moving rangers.

"Look, up ahead, what's that?" shouted Betty with nervous glee.

"It's light!" shouted Eloi. "Run to it!"

They had finally spotted the edge of the mushroom forest, about forty yards away still. But the Vampire-rats were right upon them now, some nipping at their heels. Others were climbing the mushrooms and jumping down at them. One of the rats reached out and grabbed Betty by the hair. She screamed. Jett shot it, but partly singed her hair.

"Watch it!" she yelled.

"I'll just leave the next one, then! Shall I?"

Jett and Eloi kept firing as fast as they could pull triggers. The dead rats were piling up behind them as they ran, but more and more kept flooding over the top of the dead, gnashing and biting at the rangers.

The pathway grew brighter and brighter as they ran to the edge of the light. Betty glanced behind her. The ground was a rolling carpet of red glowing eyes, reflecting in the light, and long, white fangs, hissing and snarling from rabid, foaming mouths.

They started flailing their arms frantically to dislodge the rats that were now landing on their backs and shoulders. Betty screamed again. Eloi even hollered in disgust when one bit at his hair and slobbered on his ear.

In a final, desperate leap, they were all three in the direct light of Mars' morning sun. The Vampire-rats hissed and growled at them from the safe confines of the forest shadows.

"We made it," said Eloi, huffing, with his hands on his knees.

Jett dropped his pistol while banging what looked like his arm against a rock. "Get off! Get off!" he yelled. A Vampire-rat had clenched onto his sleeve, jerking and clawing at him, its teeth violently gnashing.

Betty picked up his pistol. "I'll get it!"

"No no no no no!" shouted Jett. "Don't shoot!" He was afraid she would hit him instead.

"Stop moving!" she said, trying to aim.

"If I stop moving," he grunted, "I'm lunch!"

"Hold on!" Eloi reached into his moccasin-boot and came up with his hand, stabbing the rat against the rock, with what looked to be a long, hand-made Bowie knife.

Jett blinked at Eloi and panted a hard sigh. "Thanks."

Eloi gave a dignified nod in return, wiped the blade off on the bottom of his boot, and returned it to its hidden scabbard.

"They're not coming after us in the sunlight," said Betty.

"That's one of the reasons they're called *Vampire-rats*," Eloi responded.

"Were you bitten, Jett?" she asked.

Jett checked his shredded sleeve, then turned his arm, inspecting it. "No. But they sure played murder on my jacket."

———

It was mid-morning. The three rangers stumbled their way up the steep, rocky slope of the crater rim and stood at the edge's crest, surveying the panoramic landscape before them. Off to the east, in the haze of the distant Martian desert, indications of enormous irrigation canals were barely discernible, distributing water from the planet's vast polar ice caps to the various mushroom crops, sheltered in the widely dispersed craters across the desert's surface. To the west, near the crater rim, stood towering, monolithic rock pillars with strange alien features carved along the side, near the top.

"Are those what I think they are?" asked Betty. "They're very … totem-looking."

"Close," said Eloi. "Kruecks, are what the Martians call them. Ancient deities erected to watch over the mushroom farms within the craters. In times past, each Krueck would be adorned with hundreds of primitive ritual masks, painted and fashioned from the pelvic bones of conquered enemies."

"Barbaric," whispered Betty.

"Yes," Eloi continued. "A practice that hasn't been observed in a few generations. But only because of lack of opportunity, not willingness. Whatever opinions you've formed about Martians based on your encounter with Melvin, forget them. The great majority are a brutal and insidiously crafty lot. Given the opportunity, each and every pillar around this globe would be smothered with these 'masks of spoil' once again."

From the base of the crater's steep outer rim stretched a wide expanse of barren landscape, dotted sparsely with strangely exotic alien weeds, native to the arid environment.

In slightly less than two Martian hours, the rangers had reached the transit post pointed out by Gus before landing. It was a minimal structure, like a rural bus stop, standing monumentally against a flat, barren sea of red sand and stone. A raggedy, mono-laned trail drew a line next to it and disappeared on the horizon. The post was a small platform rising about ten feet up, accessed by tiny steps from the back.

Eloi studied the trail as it led up to the post. "It appears that a transport travels this route twice a day. From the looks of it, the last one came through sometime late yesterday."

"How can you tell?" asked Betty. "It only looks like a shallow, windswept ditch to me."

Eloi tilted his head and cracked a sympathetic smile. "The rangers do teach tracking, in a limited way," he said. "But, since I was very young, I learned from my people what to look for, beyond the obvious. Sadly, it's becoming a lost art."

———————

The three travelers snoozed on the ground in the shrinking shadow of the transit post for several hours. Even though the temperature was quite cool, it wasn't wise to be exposed to the sun for too long because of the thin Martian atmosphere. Periodically, Eloi ascended the stairs and scanned the horizon with his field glasses. The Martian sun was at high noon when his voice broke the silence and stirred the two dozing below. "Alright, here we go." He stowed the glasses in his satchel.

Jett and Betty joined Eloi atop the post and squinted south. A faint billowing cloud traced a line in the distance, growing fractionally larger by the second. Shortly, the approaching cloud produced a sound that began as a low rumble and grew into a symphony of metallic rattles and squeaks as the lumbering iron wheeler drew near. Wheelers were a form of Martian public transit in rural areas, primarily used for transporting agricultural attendants from cities to farms and back again.

The wheeler looked like a single giant iron tractor wheel, about forty feet in diameter, covered completely in a crusty, brownish-red corrosion. The main bus cabin was rectangular and box-like, surrounded by round, bulbous windows, with an enclosed limb that stuck out of the side for the robot driver. The cabin balanced in the center of the giant wheel by a web of tensioned coil springs and hydraulic suspension, just above a proton-drive engine that was in dire need of a tune-up.

The robot pilot drew the wheeler up to the post and pulled a brake lever, triggering a piercing screech that brought the machine to a grinding halt. An oval door on the side slid open, allowing the three Earthlings to enter, squatting and carefully ducking their heads to fit.

Two Martians sitting in the back appeared quite anxious and began whispering to each other, taking extra care not to make eye contact with the Earthlings, who were now sitting uncomfortably in the tiny Martian seats with their knees to their chests. The wheeler jolted forward and steadily rolled down the road in the direction of the Martian capital city of Füro.

CHAPTER SEVEN

ESCAPE

Jett checked his watch. Travel along the rustic path was generally rough, with occasional potholes slamming the occupants against their seats. Half an hour seemed more like two, sitting in the cramped bus. His back ached and his neck was becoming stiff. The robot pilot threw a lever that extended shiny titanium bars from each side of the wheeler's fuselage as it approached the upward sloping rim of a massive crater.

With no announcement or warning from the pilot, the wheeler immediately dropped out of sight into an unassuming hole, where its path dead-ended at the base of the crater wall. The motion of the wheeler transitioned from the noisy jolting and jarring of its rugged ride to instantaneous smoothness and extreme acceleration as the two titanium bars magnetically rolled the wheeler between two tubular tracks, which descended straight down into a vast blackness. The stomachs of all three rangers caught in their throats with an upward surge for the duration of the long freefall. The track sharply swooped horizontally and leveled off. An increasing bevy of lights began whizzing past the windows from an underground city that expanded to breathtaking proportions in all directions.

The city of Füro had one thick beam of natural sunlight that highlighted its downtown, open to the sky above from the center of the giant crater. Its sky-scraping spires stretched upward, reaching for the rim of the crater from far below. The rest of the city extended many layers down into the pit and in all directions horizontally, like a giant underground ant colony. An eerie lime fluorescence glowed from city lights in the shadowed sections, creating a sense of surrealism to the viewer who was unaccustomed to its effect.

The familiar shrieking of metal upon metal pierced the air as the brakes were applied again and the wheeler came to a halt at one of the city's transit stations. As soon as the Earthlings exited, the two Martians in back scrambled through the door and quickly scurried away, glancing over their shoulder several times before disappearing into the crowd.

"We don't exactly blend in, do we?" said Betty, as she noticed that they were at least twice as tall as the tallest Martian in the busy terminal.

Eloi motioned to Jett. "Martian police at nine o'clock." He quickly scanned the area for others.

"They've already seen us," said Betty.

"We can't afford to be detained here by the authorities," said Eloi. "Mars is very corrupt politically, and law is determined by the whim of the local warlord in charge. Quickly, this way."

They ducked into a narrow passageway where they could get

away from the crowd, zigzagging their way through back streets. Usually, it is easy to get lost in a crowd, but when one stands as a giant among the locals, it is best to keep to the shadows and lesser-traveled avenues.

Jett stopped abruptly and grabbed the other two by the sleeves. "This way." He ducked left around a corner.

They waited and listened. There were many footsteps up ahead. The authorities who had spotted them at the terminal were now trying to cut them off.

"We do know where we're going, right?" asked Betty.

"Melvin's info was helpful," said Eloi. "But it could have been a bit more detailed. It's been a while since I've been here, and things have changed a little."

Betty frowned. "I don't know how you can be so comfortable, putting your trust in that Martian."

"You never know what a lead is worth until you check it out," said Jett.

The sound of the footsteps dissipated in the other direction.

Eloi stepped out into the street. "Keep moving." He led the way.

"What happens if we don't find what we're looking for?" asked Betty.

"You rarely find what you're looking for," said Jett. "Most of the time, you just hope to find something that's not a dead end."

"Well, that sounds right." Betty rolled her eyes. "It does feel like we're just running till we hit something most of the time."

They moved quietly down a darkened alley when Eloi motioned with his hand for them to stop.

"Do you hear that?" he whispered to Jett.

Jett strained to listen, then finally nodded. Eloi pointed to an alcove in the wall to the right, and the three made themselves disappear in the shadowed recess. As a skilled tracker himself, Jett was thoroughly impressed by the old man's keen senses.

It seemed they had managed to lose the authorities who had been chasing them, and this new group of footsteps appeared to be just some local Martian hoodlums roaming the streets. Moments later, eight of them rounded a corner. One was practicing flipping a knife in the air as he walked and catching it again by the handle before it hit the ground. He did this a few times as they approached. He flipped it another time and missed, allowing it to fall to the ground and bounce several times before it rolled to a stop, just a few inches from Jett's foot.

While two in the small gang were roughing on one of the others in horseplay, the knife-twirler casually walked over to the wall to retrieve his dropped blade. The Martian half bent to snag it and jumped back with a startled yelp when he noticed the three Earthlings hiding in the shadow.

Jett calmly reached down to pick up the knife and handed it to the Martian with a smile.

"Here ya go. Sorry about that. We were looking for the quachi and made a wrong turn somewhere along the way. Would you be so kind as to point us in the right direction?" Quachi means restroom in Martian; Jett did know a few of their words.

Five of the Martians drew weapons, and they all began to make a semicircle around the rangers, who were now pinned against the wall. Because of the dark shadow, the Martians couldn't see the ranger uniforms; they could only tell that they were Earthlings. And they couldn't see that Jett and Eloi were armed.

One Martian uttered in very broken English something that sounded like, "Prepare to die," followed by "Earthlings," which was understood very clearly. The Martians raised their weapons as if to fire.

The street lit up with a flash and the sound of rapid-fire laser.

Five Martians lay dead in the street. A hint of smoke trailed up from the barrel of Jett's drawn pistol.

Eloi was impressed. "You have a talent there, my boy, to be sure. I don't think I've ever seen anyone so quick. You popped those mugs before I could even clear leather."

The other three Martians were caught flat-footed. Two looked scared, and Jett was keeping a close watch on the shifty-eyed one to the left, the one who had tried to draw but waited too late. That kind are very unpredictable and will sometimes try anything foolish and desperate when cornered.

"Now I hope the three of you chaps are quite a bit more hospitable than your friends over here," said Jett sarcastically. "All we want is just a little information. First, though, why don't you very delicately put your weapons on the ground and kick them over here."

Eloi translated for him into Martian, but it didn't sound as polite. The guns were kicked over.

Betty bent and picked one of them up.

"The handle is a bit small for me, but I think this will do." She tucked it under her belt behind her back.

Eloi stepped forward and uttered something in Martian. Jett and Betty didn't understand any of it, except the word "Rog," which brought a flash of surprise to the eyes of the interrogatees.

As expected, there was no response from the Martians, at least nothing helpful. The shifty-eyed one kept nervously glancing up to the rooftops above the rangers, which made Jett even more uneasy. Was it a ploy to get him to look away for an instant, so the Martian could make a move? Was there something up there? Or was he expecting something to be up there?

Across the street, there was a door slightly ajar that led into what appeared to be an empty warehouse of some kind. Jett motioned to Eloi and Betty. "Let's get these fellas off the street. We're too exposed out here. I don't like it."

Eloi agreed.

Inside the warehouse was a large, dark room with an arched ceiling and a smooth, slick floor. Jett glanced around; the best he could tell about the building, in the thick darkness, was that it was a reappropriated space ship hangar. Once inside, their footsteps echoed as if in a large cavernous, chamber with thick rock walls.

Eloi wasted no time with the Martians and continued to see what information he could get out of them. He wasn't nearly as pleasant now as he was with Melvin. Even if he had coconuts to bargain with, it seems that he would not have wasted them on these three.

Betty stepped close to Jett and whispered in his ear, "He seems awfully sure these three can tell us something. Why is that? Is he just guessing, or is there something I missed?"

"Because of their weapons," replied Jett. "The only ones with weapons like this on Mars, especially of this quality, are the authorities and the mafia. And generally, the gray line is pretty dim dividing the two."

Betty was impressed by the simple deduction. Of course, the answer seemed obvious to her now, after Jett had explained it, but she wasn't sure she would have come to that on her own. She hoped that over time she would become as skillful at assessing a situation.

There was a noise in the darkness. "What was that?" Betty quickly muttered.

They all heard it. A distinctive metal-upon-metal click in the distance.

"I don't think I like that sound," said Betty very quietly.

Jett paused a moment, then whispered, "Me neither."

Just as Betty withdrew her newfound pistol, a bright spotlight shone down on the rangers from directly above. The three Martians snickered. One of them spat on Eloi's boot; then all three backed away, leaving the rangers by themselves in the spotlight.

Dim lights around the perimeter of the chamber glowed brighter, revealing silhouetted figures of Martian men standing shoulder to shoulder on a balcony above, making a complete circle around the outer wall of the large chamber. They methodically stomped their feet in unison, creating the effect of a primitive drumbeat, announcing the onset of eminent doom. Each had a laser rifle drawn and ready, giving the rangers no hope of escape. All of them wore masks of painted human pelvic bones.

The rangers holstered their pistols. Try as they might, they could think of no way out, as they stood back-to-back below the encircling ring of executioners. At this point, they knew a gunfight was not advisable; the odds were too stacked against them.

A small, oval-shaped hover-platform eased past the rim of the balcony. A black-gloved hand went up, and the stomping immediately ceased, leaving a rolling echo that trailed around the metallic cavern. A sharply dressed Martian stood proud, left hand gripping the front rail of the hover-platform, the other still in the air, commanding silence. He wore a black pin-striped suit with familiar Earth-style tailoring, but still very Martian in its styling. His head looked like a giant bullfrog with fat lips; atop his head, two antennae stuck out of the top of a derby hat. Various old scars crisscrossed his face, one notably deep scar carving a shadowy, jagged line from under his hat, over his left eye, and up under his jaw. He slowly rolled a short, fat stump of a cigar from one side of his mouth to the other. A bodyguard stood on the hover-platform just behind him with rifle drawn.

"Rog," Eloi spat.

Betty glanced at Jett.

"How polite of you to send out the welcoming party," said Eloi. "And who says Martians don't know hospitality?"

Rog stood silently, staring down at the rangers, studying them. Finally, he snorted and, with much effort, spoke with a small voice that came from the back of his throat and wasn't much more than a loud whisper. "You. Old one. You look familiar."

A smile slowly broke across Eloi's stoic expression. "Come now, dear fellow. I'm not one to ring my own bell, but I thought I left a stronger impression than this." He paused for a moment to let the Martian think. "I'm the cosmetic surgeon who improved your ugly appearance, long ago."

Rog unconsciously raised a gloved hand to his scar and caressed it. "Yes." The skin at the corners of his eyes and mouth tightened. "As they say on Earth, revenge is sweet." He raised his hand once more. "And you brought friends. More entertaining."

He dropped his hand, and the floor began to slowly sink below the rangers' feet. They were standing in the center of a large circular section that had been released by what sounded like a gravity-lock brake, which allowed gears to slowly ratchet the trap floor downward with a metallic *click click click*. As they descended, the clanking began to get louder and grow in rapidity, but the floor was not lowering any faster. The sound was no longer metallic, but rather organic.

A sudden realization hit Jett. "Sting-adders—a whole pit of them."

Light glinted off oily black scales, undulating like a rolling sea of serpentine fingers reaching up to them. Venomous viper heads struck at the air in anticipation. Long tails with scorpion-like stingers swayed hypnotically, then whipped, ready to strike. Giant, crab-like pincers clicked rapidly, mimicking the sound of a rattlesnake den.

Betty peered over the edge. The floor was not visible; there were so many. Her stomach sank. She turned to Jett. "What do we do?" she shrieked.

"Don't panic," said Jett.

That was easy for him to say, she thought. The Martians above began their rhythmic stomping again.

Jett reached into his pocket and threw the piece of circuit board on the floor in front of him.

Rog stared at the electronic component for a few moments then slowly raised his hand again. The stomping ceased.

Betty scrutinized Jett. He was up to something but had yet to figure out what. She was amazed that, in the face of death, he was able to stand there like a pillar, as if he was in total control of the situation and had no doubts about it. This was one of those moments she had read so much about but had yet to experience—the bravery of rangers in an impossible situation. Her mind quickly reflected on how many times they had escaped death in just the past few days, and here she was, still alive.

But for how long?

This exhibition of bravery intrigued Rog, and he moved his hover-platform closer to get a better look at the circuit panel.

"I believe this belongs to you," said Jett.

Rog rolled his cigar stump to the other side of his mouth and began chewing on it. "So," he said with slight amusement, "you found one of my little gifts to planet Earth." He removed something resembling a gold pocket watch and glanced at it. "Very soon these remote-controlled toys are going to change the balance of many things. A great show it will be." He frowned at the rangers. "But not for you."

Betty stepped forward. "Whatever this pathetic little plan of yours is, Mr. Scar-Toad, the rangers will squash it." She glanced at Jett and whispered, "Right?"

"Ahh," replied Rog, with great satisfaction. "Now that's the beauty of it all, Miss Rangerita. At zero hour, the conductor of this whole orchestra will be directing from the very core of your kind."

The sound of the sting-adders below was becoming increasingly louder as the floor sank lower and lower.

Jett shook his head. "You're not going to get away with this. As a matter of fact, this stops right here."

Rog rolled his cigar once more, relishing every moment. "You will die, right here."

"And the funny thing is," said Jett, "you yourself are going to save us from this pit."

Rog's amusement was piqued. He grinned big and laughed, quietly nodding his head, as he turned to some Martians on his left, most of whom gave no response because very few Martians understood the language being spoken.

"Enough yip-yap," said Jett. "You're a boring conversationalist anyway."

In a flash, Jett's pistol was drawn. Two shots were fired so fast, they seemed like one. The first shot hit the bodyguard's gun, exploding it in his hand. The second hit the rear motor of the hover-platform, sending it careening into the edge of the opposite balcony. The jolt dislodged Rog from his perch and sent him tumbling down to the floor below, where he landed flat on his stomach at the rangers' feet.

Eloi wasted no time and immediately grabbed him by the scruff of the neck and had his knife at the mob boss' throat. The bodyguard clung to the ship's railing until it hit the edge of the descending floor. He was thrown free and fell to the sting-adders below.

The bodyguard wailed in agony. The sting-adders swarmed over him until he was completely covered in a rolling shimmy of black scales. Some bit with their fangs, some struck with their tails and stung him, while others pinched his flesh away with their tearing and gnashing claws.

The Martians above were stunned and confounded. Their weapons were all trained on the rangers once again, but one shot from any of them and Eloi would split their leader wide open. The tables were turned. But the descending platform was about to reach bottom, where a painful death still awaited.

Betty gasped when the swarm opened for a second to reveal the bodyguard's face. It was twice as big as normal and swollen to a dark purple with bright red bumps all over. Soon, the bodyguard would be dead—suffocated by his own swelling body. There was nothing anyone could do for him now. Betty's eyes got big. She grimaced and looked away quickly.

Rog's eyes were red, and he was coughing, choking. Jett stepped over and slapped him hard on the back. The little stump of a cigar dislodged and came flying out of his mouth, bouncing on the floor.

"I know you've got a contingency plan; tell them to use it, or you die with us."

"I'm not afraid to die," said Rog, still coughing.

Jett looked at him and snorted. "Then an entertaining show we'll have, indeed."

Thumps, scratching, and clawing came from under the floor as the sting-adders began striking from below.

Rog thought hard then finally relented. He waved his hand. "Spray 'em."

Several of the creatures started climbing on the descending

floor with them. Jett and Betty shot the closest ones. Eloi held the knife steady at Rog's throat.

"Spray 'em!" Rog yelled, this time a distinct squeak in his voice. Rog was one of the toughest of his breed, but he wanted desperately to live to fight these rangers another day.

A green gas was injected into the lower room from all directions. It had no effect on the rangers or the Martian, but it began to sedate the sting-adders and finally put them to sleep. There was a service entrance on the wall with a hermetically sealed door that was never locked. There was no need—no one ever survived long enough to reach it. With the green fog now obscuring the rangers' actions from the Martians above, Jett fired a few blasts at the floor and cleared a path. Scales, giant bug legs, and snake parts flew to the left and right.

Jett spun the crank that opened the door. "Let's go!"

Betty swiftly followed. Eloi brought up the rear and pushed Rog ahead. They ran down a short hallway, took some stairs that led to a lower level, and found themselves in the entrance of what looked like a maintenance area, which opened up to a much larger room. Steam ventilation tubes, sewer pipes, and electrical wires ran everywhere along the ceiling and walls.

Jett turned to face the rest. "We've got to get outta here." He pointed his gun at Rog. "But we can't trust *him* to tell us how."

Rog stood defiant and slowly shook his head. "You won't escape."

There was a scattered series of loud booms. All exits were

instantly sealed by thick fire doors slamming to the floor. Eloi was still on the other side; he hadn't stepped through the opening of the last door yet. They were cut off.

Betty beat on the door with her fists. "Eloi! Can you hear me?"

There was nothing. The metal slab was much too thick.

"See?" Rog smiled. "When the rest of my gang catch up with you, I will kill you myself."

Betty jerked her head around. "You're one of those types who needs a crowd backing you up to be tough. You're nothing now."

Rog considered her for a moment, then turned to Jett. "I like her. She's funny."

"One wrong move from you"—Jett trained his gun on Rog—"and you're pork roast."

Something caught Betty's eye. A movement, a shadow, she wasn't sure. She glanced at Jett.

"I saw it," he said.

"What was that?"

Jett slowly shook his head. He stood motionless and trained his ears for any sound that seemed out of the ordinary. A low hum of machinery seemed to come from rooms beyond, along with dripping now and then from pipes snaking the ceiling and walls. Lighting was poor. If a person let their imagination get carried away, they could begin to see all kinds of creatures lurking in the shadows, waiting, ready to pounce.

But Betty saw it too, and Jett's well-seasoned instincts told him he wasn't mistaken about what he saw—the briefest shadow of a humanoid figure slinking high across the left wall. They mustn't linger long, he knew this. The place would soon be crawling with angry Martians seeking to avenge the humiliating insult thrust upon their leader. Time was not on their side. And what was that glint of a shadow that moved before them, by the catwalk overhead? He looked around. "There's gotta be a way outta here."

A smile that better resembled a mad dog's snarl cracked across Rog's features. "This place is in lock-down" His voice strained. "Only my boys can get in or out. They will search each room one by one until they find us. You put on an interesting show, ranger, but you're wasting time. You were lucky ... and foolish. This is my territory. When this is over, I will take special pride in having my new war mask fashioned from your bones." He glanced at Betty. "Both of you. I might even have a special necklace made for my niece from your teeth."

Jett moved close to Rog. "What else is in here with us?"

Rog simply continued smiling, revealing a few worn, yellow, stumpy teeth.

A high-pitched cry that sounded half like a scream and half like a howl filled the chamber, echoing as it trailed off. Hair stood up on the back of the rangers' necks.

Eyes wide, Betty turned to Jett. "I don't like the sound of that."

A black shadow swiftly moved toward them from the platform above. It jumped and gracefully spun through the air, nailing a sure-footed landing about a stone's throw in front of them. Cloaked in black, a humanoid figure stood before them and moved into an aggressive stance, obviously preparing for a duel. Its skin was the deepest ebony and glistened in the dim light of this lower chamber. Its eyes were solid white with no apparent pupils, giving it an almost ghost-like appearance. The creature flicked a button on a tube-like device it was holding in its hand, and a thin sword instantaneously telescoped from the handle and clicked into place. With a flick of its wrist, the creature spun the sword so fast that it made the sound of a giant propeller. It stepped forward, stuck out its chest, and roared like a lion, producing a high-pitched shriek that could almost break glass. Its many teeth were sharp and pointed like a shark's.

Betty realized Rog had slipped away. "Where's Rog?"

Jett spun; the Martian mob boss was gone. He gritted his teeth. "Great."

The creature took another step and bounded high in the air, spinning toward the two rangers, its thin, polished blade flashing reflected light as it came.

Jett very calmly raised his pistol and fired a laser blast at the creature. It effortlessly deflected the blast, with its mirror-finish sword, before landing about ten feet in front of them.

Jett took a few steps backward. "Oh, boy."

Jett rapidly fired a few more times, but the creature deflected the blasts as if they were simply playing a game. Jett knew now that this was the creature that had produced the results of the photos that he had seen in Director Freder's office. He was now facing the mysterious Space Ranger killer, and if he didn't think of something fast, he and Betty would be the next victims.

"Betty!" he yelled. "Let's fire at the same time; we'll see how quick this thing really is."

Both rangers sent several blasts simultaneously, but the creature had lightning-fast reflexes and deflected them, seemingly exactly where it wanted the blasts to land. The creature could have very easily deflected the laser blasts back at the rangers and been done with them, but after seeing the photos of the murdered rangers and how they had been sliced up like sausages, Jett knew that the creature wanted the pleasure of killing the rangers with its own sword and not by merely returning the rangers' own fire back at them.

The two rangers quickly backpedaled and smashed against the locked fire door. There was now nowhere to go. The creature's sword vigorously whirred in the air as it stepped forward to deliver the final death blow.

Betty screamed, and the creature bared its teeth and squalled once more, drowning out her frightened voice. Jett quickly fired a blast at the wall next to their attacker, exploding a pressurized steam pipe and violently hurling the creature across the room to their left.

He grabbed Betty's hand and tugged as they ran. "Quick!" They reached the other end of the long room before the creature had gotten back to its feet. Jett searched the wall along the floor.

"It's got to be somewhere over here." He waved his hand in front of a series of vented panels.

"What are you doing?" Betty looked behind them, gun ready.

"I felt a draft a while ago," said Jett. "It had to come from over here." He stopped abruptly. "Bingo. Here we go." He opened a grille cover and threw it to the floor.

"Congratulations," said Betty. "You found the air conditioner."

Jett grunted as he tugged at the second panel, ripping it open. "Martians don't have air conditioning. They use convection." He threw the panel aside. "This should lead out."

The creature howled and came flying out of the shadows again, with blade held high.

"Keep it busy for a second while I get this open," Jett shouted.

Betty fired at the creature a few more times, which did little good. It bared its teeth again and seemed to enjoy the resistance the rangers offered as it sent a laser volley just over Betty's head, exploding sparks from the electrical panels on the wall by Jett.

"Aaargh!" Jett rubbed his arm to shed the burning sparks. He looked through the crawl space that led outside. It was sealed with iron bars, which he blasted free with a few quick shots. "Come on, Betty!" he yelled.

Betty crawled through the short tunnel about five feet and came to an opening in the outer wall that dropped off many stories down to another level below. A monorail next to the building carried a Martian commuter train toward them. Jett stood guard at the opening and fired a few more frivolous shots at the creature.

"There's a train coming!" exclaimed Betty.

"Good!" Jett yelled. "Jump!"

Betty looked down. The monorail track was a good two stories below the opening. It would be at least a story-and-a-half drop to the top of the train, and if she missed, there was a much longer drop to the ground below. The train wasn't really moving very fast yet, but to Betty, it might as well have been a speeding bullet. Her heart began to race, and her hands started sweating.

"I'm not sure I can do this," she said to herself.

Jett ducked into the crawl space with Betty as the train began passing by below. "Jump!"

Betty's breath was short and fast; she hesitated.

Jett put his hand on her back. "If you don't jump, I'll push! Jump! Jump now!"

She put her foot on the edge of the opening and jumped. Strangely, she began counting to herself as she fell. One, two. Thud! The top of the train was smooth and slightly rounded. She lost her footing and went spread-eagle, face down. Her gun slipped from her hand and slid over the edge. It was gone. She could have kicked herself. She knew she should have securely tucked it away before jumping. For an instant, she dreaded the conversation she would have with Jett about this later.

Jett landed several feet behind her, rolled onto his back, and drew his pistol. The creature was quick to follow, and Jett fired several more shots, hoping to catch a moment where the skilled assassin would let its guard down. But no such luck. The creature deftly landed a few cars behind and began spinning his blade, moving it to the left and right as he deflected Jett's vain attempts to score a body shot.

Betty glanced forward, then yelled back to Jett, "Tunnel!"

Jett jerked his head to glimpse the hole in the rock wall beginning to swallow the train. The creature sprinted toward them at full speed, furiously flinging its sword left and right. Jett and Betty flattened themselves tight against the top of the train. If the creature didn't get to the rangers before their car made the tunnel, it would have to bail off, since it required adequate room to move its sword to deflect the laser blasts. Jett fired as fast as he could to keep the creature busy. The creature was right in front of Jett. It howled and jumped, with sword poised for attack.

Jett gasped and reflexively flinched. Everything went black.

CHAPTER EIGHT

BLADE OF THE ASSASSIN

Betty wanted to reach out in the dark for Jett but was afraid of what she would find. Everything happened so quickly before they entered the tunnel, and she wasn't exactly sure what she saw. The droning of the monorail and the wind in the tunnel made a sound like a loud, breathy whistle, similar to an old house in a windstorm. She felt cold. Did the creature land his blow, or did he miss?

She stretched out a trembling hand into the dark and blindly groped until she felt the tuft of Jett's hair.

"Are you O.K., Jett?"

Jett grabbed her wrist. "Yeah, it jumped off at the last minute!" he yelled back to her through the noisy wind. "That was too close for comfort!"

She closed her eyes in relief for a moment, then opened them again. Light. They had passed through to the other side.

———

Jett and Betty sat on some rusted canisters behind the monorail depot at the edge of town. They had slipped off the top of the train and sneaked behind the hangars when the afternoon conductor had stopped to switch shifts. Their ride hadn't taken them very far, maybe only a few miles from where they had jumped on the train. Jett reached down and rubbed his ankle.

"How are you holding up?" asked Betty.

"Could be better. That jump was a little farther than I anticipated."

They had found a hidden place behind a junked boxcar that had been overturned and heavily picked over for spare parts. It sufficiently concealed their position from any wandering eyes over by the depot. It was a good place to rest, where they could catch their breath, reflect on the recent events, and decide their next steps. A strange-looking, mangy creature darted from under the heap—the Martian equivalent of a stray cat.

Now that Jett finally had a quiet moment to mentally digest all that had recently transpired, many things began to press his mind. From the not-so-subtle hints that Rog had given, there were obviously more of those awful robots on Earth. Worker robots equipped for war. Did the people receiving these robots know what they were getting? Or were they unsuspecting pawns, used for distributing Trojan horses throughout the city that could be remotely activated to turn against their masters? But for what purpose? Whatever it was, it was supposed to happen very soon.

And what of the cryptic message, *At zero hour, they will be directed from the core of your kind?* This made no sense to Jett. He needed to think. He had no idea of the time frame involved in these events, but there was an urgency to send a warning. He needed to get word back to Ranger Headquarters, to alert them of … of what? That was the question. What exactly was going on here? Would these Martians be so bold as to try to invade? The thought seemed ridiculous but still troubling. He had seen only the small pieces of evidence of a larger scheme that was being plotted. But by whom, and to what end?

Jett's mind also turned to Eloi. Did he make it out O.K.? Was he able to escape? He was an experienced old veteran, with quite a few sneaky tricks up his sleeve. Jett wondered if he would ever see him again.

He looked at Betty. Why was she here? Why was he assigned a partner to take on this mission? Jett liked working alone. It was safer. When two travel together, one isn't as sharp as he would be if he were alone. When you're alone, your senses are keener; your eyes pick up things normally missed, subtle movement in the distance, hearing is more attuned, instinct is more alert. Two people traveling together are distracted by each other; they let their guard down, each relying on the alertness of the other, and thus, the attention of both combined is less than one ranger traveling alone. Jett was used to traveling alone and felt clumsy dragging this young woman along, having to teach her the ropes while trying to solve one of his most difficult and dangerous cases. What was the director thinking? And why now, of all times?

A ranger was never assigned to a mission like this straight out of the academy. The young ones would cut their teeth on things like corporate corruption and border disputes, certainly not ranger assassinations. Could this be the brainchild of the Oversight Committee chairman? Could that clown have orchestrated this?

Was this punishment for the mess Jett made on the moon? Surely not. He had done worse than that before with merely a slap on the wrist. But he always got the job done. Maybe it wasn't always textbook clean, but the job got done. The case got solved, and most importantly, when a case was assigned to Captain Jethro Rogers, the deeds of the guilty would always find their judgment. He was just one in a long line of defenders of justice, a blunt instrument wielded to defend those who have no defense. Strength and courage pulsed through his veins, which compelled him to stand under circumstances that would cause a normal man to cower in fear. He would not back down from his duty, and he would not leave Eloi behind.

The thought had just snapped into his mind. Yes, Eloi was an experienced ranger. He knew what he was getting into, but he was here because he was helping Jett, and Jett was now determined that he would not return to the ship without him.

He twisted the top of his wrist watch, flicked it open, and pressed a few small buttons. "Let's go," he said sharply.

"What is that?" asked Betty.

"It's like a compass." Jett showed her the face of the instrument. "It was my grandfather's. It can remember the coordinates of where you've been and direct you how to get back. It doesn't need satellite support to work. Very much like a compass, it uses a planet's magnetic field. It's come in handy several times. I set it back at Rog's hideout. We're going back for Eloi."

Betty's eyes registered concern, and her face seemed to lose some color. She swallowed hard and rose to follow. She wasn't keen on going back to the lair of Rog, but deep inside she knew it was the proper thing to do, and the strength that comes from knowing you're doing right seemed to rise up inside her and compel her forward.

————

They followed a primitive path that weaved close to the rocky edge of the inner crater wall until they came across a large, grated vent. Jett scanned the area to make sure there was no one who would hear his blast and fired a few times, obliterating the lock. The two rangers slid the metallic covering aside and mounted a small ladder that descended down the long cold shaft into the darkness.

Their steps echoed and breath was amplified as the air around them grew blacker and blacker.

"Obviously, you have a plan," said Betty. "Where are we going? Where will this take us?"

"Füro is built on top of a much older ruined city, which is not much more than a connected series of catacombs now, vented like this throughout the city for drainage and access to subterranean utilities. We'll use these catacombs to approach Rog's hideout from below. And we won't have to interact with any of the locals to get there."

"And this *compass* of yours will guide us?"

"You got it."

"Have you ever been down here before?" she asked.

"Nope."

"And you're sure we can get where we want to go?"

"One way or another."

"Flying by the seat of your pants seems to be this guy's life philosophy," she muttered to herself.

It took several minutes to reach bottom. The air was cold, damp, and musty and had the smell of undisturbed age. Jett produced a small flashlight from a pocket inside his jacket. It illuminated their path and cast ghostly shadows along uneven walls as they passed and disappeared into a black nothing above, with the exception of a few glimmers of giant arches here and there. The ceiling was vaulted high and curved like a giant cathedral. Upon closer inspection, the ceiling and walls seemed to be made of a soft, organic substance rather than rock.

Betty reached out and touched it. "It's hard as rock, but it looks like wood."

"Petrified roots of giant trees, now extinct to this planet," replied Jett.

"I didn't know there was evidence of those things still in existence."

"Very few Earthlings have ever been down here," he said. "And not in a long while. My grandmother told me about them, from stories she had heard from my grandfather. Evidently, he had been down here too."

"They must have been enormous," she whispered. "Larger than the mushrooms. Much larger, in fact."

They walked silently for what seemed like a mile, each quietly keeping their thoughts to themselves, when Betty eventually spoke up. "My brother."

"What?"

"A while back, when you asked why someone like me would join the corps ... it was because of my brother." She took a deep breath as they walked, glanced ponderously around the dark cavern, and continued. "He was several years older than me when it happened. I was still just a little girl at the time. He worked on a trans-planetary barge. His run was from several of the moons of Jupiter back to Earth. The transport company that he worked for gradually became plagued by raids from space pirates that would attack as they passed through the asteroid belt. The pirates would use a hit-and-run technique, striking quickly and returning to their hideouts in the mostly uncharted asteroids between Mars and Jupiter. The raids became so frequent that it was only a matter of time until his ship was attacked. I know my brother; he's always been a fighter and wouldn't have sat back and let someone hijack his cargo without putting up a fight. Subsequently, when his ship was finally raided, he was killed, along with the rest of the crew.

Their bodies were never found—probably just jettisoned into space.

"The sad thing is"—her voice rose a bit, and long repressed anger became more and more evident as she spoke—"the whole investigation, if you can call it that, lasted less than a week and was just swept under the rug. All the families of the victims got their insurance money from the company, but no real justice was ever served. It was like my brother didn't even matter, at least to the lazy, bureaucratic authorities involved at the time. Cowards! They didn't want to 'embarrass' the Martians, since it was so close to their sector."

Jett stopped and turned off the light.

"What is it?" asked Betty.

"Did you hear something?" he whispered. "That. There it is again."

"Yeah," she breathed, now barely audible.

He grabbed her arm, near the elbow. "Keep walking this way," he whispered. "And Betty ..."

"What?"

"I'm really sorry about your brother."

They took a few steps and then stopped to listen. Every step they took was matched by another set of footsteps, although the second set sounded much larger and heavier than theirs. Each time, the steps seemed to grow closer. Whatever was stalking them must have been really big because its stride was much larger than theirs. They groped blindly in front of them, until they came to what felt like a stalagmite. They scooted behind it. Jett shined his light in the direction of the steps.

An angry-sounding snort came from just below two glowing red eyes looming menacingly about three feet above them. Jett drew his pistol, ready to fire; Betty yelped in surprise. An instant longer and the creature stepped out in plain view and snorted loudly once more. Jett holstered his pistol and laughed quietly to himself.

"It's a Snurku. A Martian cave sloth," he said, with some tone of levity. "C'mon, he's harmless. He was just curious. I would imagine he doesn't get too many visitors down here, and the light made him sneeze when I flashed his eyes."

Betty considered the furry creature for a moment with a smile. "You're kinda cute, fella. You sure know how to give a girl goosebumps, though. Don't you know it's not nice to sneak up like that?" She then turned to follow Jett.

The lanky, three-legged creature lumbered toward the rangers as they walked away. It stretched its long neck along the top of the stalagmite and licked for insects it had sniffed with its long, furry snout.

Periodically, Jett checked his directional instrument for their location. In less than an hour, they approached the coordinates he had saved from within Rog's hideout above.

"Start looking for a way up," he said. "We're close."

Within minutes, they discovered some primitive rock steps that led upward along a curving rock wall. The steps were old, and some crumbled under their feet as they stepped, so they proceeded with caution. For about thirty feet, the narrow staircase sloped upward, then abruptly ended at a steep rock wall. From there, the trail continued upward about fifty feet, only now with small finger- and toe-holes carved into the stone long ago for a much smaller race than humans. Moisture seeped from the streets above, coating the walls with a slippery film of slime, making them hard to grip. Jett and Betty both slipped several times during their ascent and had to use the utmost care.

The precarious carved ladder finally reached a narrow plateau that ran along the edge of the wall. At the end of the plateau, a slender shaft of light beamed down and illuminated a skinny metal ladder that descended from a small, bright point—a vent—that reached the city's surface.

Jett squinted through narrow slats of the vent to the street beyond. To his dismay, there was a large crowd of Martians—a busy street market. He checked the vent; it was locked down. He couldn't risk drawing attention to himself by shooting the locks loose, yet that was the only way out. He couldn't wait until nightfall; that was too long. Time was ticking. He needed to find Eloi and get him out of there as soon as possible, then high-tail it back to the *Ares* to send a message of warning. Jett began to doubt if he shouldn't have sent the message first, then come back for Eloi.

No. He would find a way. An opportunity always avails itself, even if sometimes you have to create that opportunity for yourself.

He would wait and watch.

"What's going on up there?" asked Betty, clinging to the ladder, just below him. She could hear the noise from the street above and deduced the unlikelihood of their quick exit.

"Crowded," grumbled Jett.

Jett checked his location device again. They were close. The hideout was probably just on the other side of the wall, at street level next to the grate. Might there be another way into this mafia hideout from the catacombs? Maybe, but it would probably be hidden in such a way that the rangers would never find it. Should they go down and look for another grate? That was a possibility. But for now, they would wait. As Jett was thinking about all these things, he remembered something he wanted to ask.

"Betty?"

"Yeah?"

"On Aurora Four, who did you call?"

Her face flushed a bit. "What do you mean?"

"You know what I mean; who did you call?"

"There was no time to call anyone."

"When you went to the restroom. Only you didn't go to the restroom, you called someone. Who did you call from out there?"

She hesitated for a moment, unsure what to do. She had been instructed to keep her real reason for being there from her partner. But after all they had been through together so far, she figured Jett deserved to know the truth. "The assistant director instructed me that it was upon the director's orders that I check in whenever I could to give an update."

"Update?"

"On our progress. He said this mission was too important to him; he needed to be in the loop. And that was my primary task."

"To keep him in the loop."

"Yes."

"Why did he want you to do this?"

"I don't know. This is a bit unique, with rangers being murdered and all. Maybe he just needed to feel like he had more control of the situation. If I were the director, I would want to know what was going on out in the field."

Down the street, a trash-collection vehicle stopped to mechanically lift a large garbage bin overhead and dump it into its cargo hold and compact it, making a noisy crunching sound.

"You would, would you?" continued Jett.

"Why, yes."

"Enough to send spies along with your field rangers to tattle on their every move?"

"I don't ..." She knew she was treading in dangerous waters and decided to let it go. "I'm sorry you feel this way. I'm only following orders. The assistant director told me I shouldn't tell you what I was doing. He said you'd only get angry. But I thought you had a right to know."

"You thought I had the right to know, did you?"

"Yes."

"Then why didn't you offer this information? Why did I have to drag it out of you?"

The trash-collection vehicle had stopped nearly overhead to pick up another container. Its gears whined as it lifted its heavy load, clanging metal upon metal as it emptied its contents.

"I was only following orders." Her voice began to shake. "Surely you understand?"

"Oh, I understand, alright." He drew his pistol, eyes glaring.

Betty recoiled. "Wait!"

Jett fired rapidly three times and slid the grate open. "Come on! Let's move! Now's our chance!"

The two rangers were able to duck behind the trash container as soon as it was lowered back to its place. Quickly, Jett picked the lock on the service door, and before anyone on the street had noticed, they were inside the Martian mafia's hideout once again.

The two made their way down a long hallway and stopped at the corner to listen. There was dead silence, similar to the night before.

"This place always seems empty at first," said Betty. "What do you make of it?"

"Be careful," said Jett. "That's what I make of it." He motioned, with gun in hand, for her to follow.

They crept down a few more hallways, stopping to listen at every corner and peering into a few empty rooms along the way.

"If I didn't know any better"—Jett stopped to listen again—"I'd say they've cleared out. Still, don't let your guard down. The last thing we need is to let these Martians catch us flat-footed again."

They came to the edge of the large room where they were ambushed the night before. The two squatted down behind some boxes and surveyed the area.

"Look," whispered Betty, pointing over Jett's shoulder.

It looked like Eloi, but he was wearing Frankie's trench coat and hat. He appeared to be sneaking along the far wall, opposite the rangers. Betty wanted to get his attention, but Jett grabbed her by the belt and pulled her back.

"No," he whispered. "Wait."

"That is him, isn't it?" she asked.

They heard footsteps coming from the hallway to the left. Eloi ducked into an alcove and did something very strange. Betty put her hand over her mouth to keep from gasping out loud. Right before their eyes, they saw Eloi transform his figure into what looked like the smuggler, Frankie Malone.

Jett watched in shock. Eloi was an Oltercian!

They couldn't tell for sure, because of the distance, but when the creature started yelling at the Martians in Frankie's voice, Jett concluded, Eloi was Frankie Malone.

Jett's stomach sank. His mind reeled. This couldn't be. It didn't make sense. How could he have been fooled so utterly? He looked at Betty. Her eyes were filled with astonished disbelief. The awful feeling of betrayal had gripped them both.

A group of Martians entered the big room. Eloi, or rather, Frankie, stepped out from the alcove and confronted them. The Martians were all heavily armed and seemed very agitated about something. Frankie said something to them in the Martian tongue, and a small argument erupted between them. The argument soon ended with the group storming off one way and Frankie leaving through a door in the other direction.

"Did you catch any of that?" asked Betty, for she didn't understand most of the Martian words.

"Best I can tell," said Jett, "they're still looking for someone, and Frankie told them to go check the other wing of the complex, which the Martians weren't too inclined to do but did it anyway. Evidently, Frankie Malone has some sway over these Martians and has a bigger role to play in this whole game than I originally thought."

Jett's anger was written across his face. His hand was clenched, and his shoulders were stiff. He had been betrayed and lied to by someone he thought was a friend.

Betty put her hand on Jett's shoulder. "Oh, Jett." She shook her head.

Jett stood up with a steely glare. "We came here to get someone, and that's still exactly what we're going to do. Only now, dead or alive is fine with me. Come on!"

As they made their way through the corridors, it became clear that the place was mostly empty now. Several storage containers had been ripped open and strewn across the floor—a sign that the occupants of the hideout had vacated in haste.

"If I'm not mistaken," said Betty, "these boxes look as if they carried weaponry."

"You're not mistaken," said Jett.

He nodded, and they silently continued down the corridor. They entered another room filled with machinery and piping, similar to the one they had escaped from the night before, only this one was much larger.

"Keep your eyes peeled," said Jett.

He kept glancing up along the ceiling—this was another good place for someone to get the drop on them. Cautiously, they proceeded, keeping close to the wall. It wasn't long before they heard voices ahead. Jett raised his hand, and they stopped abruptly. Flattening themselves behind some wall-mounted utility boxes, they peered around the edge. Several yards away, Frankie Malone spoke into a hand-held communicator. Very angrily, he was telling some Martians that they were searching in the wrong place for something. He was no longer wearing his trench coat and hat.

As soon as Frankie put his communicator away, Jett stepped out into the open and drew his pistol.

"Frankie Malone, or maybe I should I say, Eloi Lightfoot? Either way, dead or alive, you're coming with me."

Frankie jumped with surprise. "What?"

Jett held his gun higher and adjusted his grip. "All this time I thought you were just a two-bit hoodlum. But now I discover that you're something even lower, even more despicable. You're a traitor!"

Frankie began to move his hands, and Jett promptly advised him to keep them up.

"You're pretty thick, copper," said Frankie, "coming here like this. You were lucky to get away once; it won't happen again. And oh ... looky here. Who's the lady friend?"

"Don't play games with me, Frankie, Eloi, or whatever your name is." Jett indicated with his pistol. "Start walking."

"I don't think this ranger business suits you, copper. It's gettin' to your head or somethin'. You know," Frankie twirled his finger near his ear, "you've always been a dirty rat, but you're talkin' crazy stuff."

Just then, they heard the familiar loud shriek. The hair on Betty's neck stood on end again. The black, sword-wielding creature that had almost killed them was back. A dark shadow swept across the floor where they were standing, and the creature dove from a hidden place above. Jett fired.

The creature spun and twisted acrobatically in the air at dizzying speed and deftly deflected the laser blast. It landed softly on the floor and spun its swords, making a loud whirring sound. It arched its back and screamed. The pitch was almost deafening and sent a chill of intimidation through the souls of its potential victims. It had two short swords, one in each hand held by its side, hilts facing down, sword tips pointing up behind its elbows, as it slowly walked toward its prey. Its breathing was heavy and sounded almost like a growl.

Jett fired again, but it was hopeless. The creature sliced through the air, deflecting the blast as if it were an annoying, slow-moving gnat. Frankie drew his pistol and moved between the rangers and the creature.

Frankie turned to the creature and put up his hand. "Stop. I want them for myself."

The creature quickly flicked one sword, spinning it in its hand, and kept moving forward.

Frankie fired at the floor in front of the creature's feet and yelled, "Look, you stupid Cuisinart blender. I said stop!" He fired again in the same place.

The creature shrieked, then leaped into the air. Light reflected dazzlingly off the metal as the swords spun in all directions. The creature landed on its feet softly again as the body of Frankie Malone fell to the floor with its head no longer attached.

"Oh, dear!" cried Betty.

Jett tugged her sleeve. "Run!" He turned and sent a few blasts toward the beast to try to distract it. He knew it wouldn't do much good, but maybe if it could buy them even a second more of time, that just might make the difference between life and death. He knew it was a risk to return. He knew there was a chance that they could run into this creature again. But at the time, the idea was worth the risk to retrieve Eloi. Now he felt extreme anger, amplified by betrayal. They say hindsight is always twenty-twenty, but now Jett felt stupid. They were lucky the first time, and Jett despised relying on luck. It was careless. And luck rarely came twice in a row.

The rangers ran. The creature took a few steps and leaped into the air again. Jett grabbed Betty's arm and pulled her into a side passage. He hit the button on the wall, latching the electronic lock on a door that swiftly slid down.

"That should buy us some time. C'mon!"

They ran to the end of the corridor to another heavy door. Betty hit the button to release the lock, but it didn't respond. Eyes of worry stared at Jett. There was a service panel near the floor beside the door. Jett blasted the panel off, exposing the guts of the wiring. The creature was slashing at the control panel of the first door. It slowly began to slide open.

Jett pointed at the control panel. "Get at those wires. Open that door!"

Jett fired at the breach below the door that was slowly nudging upward. But the creature had stepped to the side, careful not to reveal its legs.

"We need that door open, now!" yelled Jett.

"I'm trying!" she replied. "Some of these wires got fried."

The creature came through the door.

Jett resumed firing, but his blasts were deflected left and right. The creature even deflected a few of the blasts right back at him. One barely missed his head. Evidently, the ranger's shots were becoming annoying. Jett fired at the walls and ceiling, sending debris into its face, which slowed the creature momentarily. But it doubled its efforts and leaped toward them through the flying rubble. It was only a few steps from the rangers now.

"Open it!" yelled Jett.

"I'm not there yet!" she cried.

Jett raised his weapon to fire again, but a swift cross-cut from the creature sliced his pistol in half, just in front of the handle. The blade of the assassin came inches from his knuckles. The force knocked him off balance, and he fell to the floor where Betty was sitting, still trying to release the electronic lock.

The creature stood above the two rangers for a few split seconds as it prepared to dice them to shreds. It bared its sharp, white teeth, growled hideously, and readied its swords to slash.

Two loud popping sounds emanated from beside Jett. He looked at Betty. She was holding the small, two-shot Derringer that Eloi had given him—the so-called back-up that belonged to his grandfather.

The creature went to its knees in front of them. There was a small round hole the diameter of a bullet in each wafer-thin sword blade held in front of its body. Bright green blood oozed out of its chest from two separate places. The creature swayed for a few seconds, then fell over sideways, dead.

Betty held the small gun tightly in her shaking hands, still pointed in the direction where the creature had stood. Jett reached over with his left hand and gently took the gun from her.

He reached his other arm around her shoulder and gave a firm hug.

She leaned her head against his chest and tightly closed her eyes.

CHAPTER NINE

DEEP SPACE DOG-FIGHT

The two rangers trudged their way across the Martian desert once again on foot. Dusk painted the landscape with brilliant orange, burgundy, and purple. When they had walked far enough that the crater city of Füro was obscured by the foothills behind them, Jett produced a small cylinder from his pocket, flipped open the cap, and pressed a red button that was concealed inside. Betty watched him curiously.

"It's what the skipper gave me before we left ship," he said. "It's a homing beacon so they can retrieve us, as long as we're far enough from the city that the ship won't draw attention." His ankle was bothering him worse now than before. He sat down on a big rock to wait.

Betty did the same and sat quietly, keeping her thoughts to herself for several minutes. "How do you do it?" she asked suddenly.

"Do what?"

"Back there. How do you always keep it together? I'm not sure if I'm cut out for this ranger stuff after all. I was scared stiff." She clenched and twisted her hands. "Rangers are supposed to have nerves of steel, aren't they?"

Jett silently considered Betty for a moment. "Bravery doesn't always mean the lack of fear. In fact, it rarely does." He put his hand on her shoulder. "You saved our necks back there. You did fine, in my book."

"I was excited when I first heard about this accelerated program," she said. "But I had no idea it would be this intense."

"*Accelerated* program?" asked Jett. "What is that?"

"It's how I was picked to be your partner," she said. "I was told it was a new program they were experimenting with, and I would be one of the first. An early release from the academy, straight into the field."

"How early?" asked Jett.

"A little more than a year and a half."

A fast-approaching billow of dust sped toward them in the distance. The *Ares* came in low, about twenty feet above the surface but moving too fast to stop. Two Martian air speeders were trailing hard on its tail, firing aggressively, trying to bring the mustard-colored ship down.

Jett marveled at Betty. He now considered her in a whole new light. She was way too green to be thrust into the field, especially on such a dangerous mission as this. But surprisingly, she had held her own pretty well. In fact, a realization was growing that he likely would already be dead if it weren't for her, right along with the nagging suspicion that they both had intentionally been set up for failure.

The *Ares* darted past. The side door was open, and a small bundle was pushed out and plummeted to the sand below, landing a short distance away.

"I'll get it." Betty sprinted off.

The *Ares* rolled a hard left and darted for the canyons beyond, taking more evasive maneuvers.

Jett scanned their surroundings and noticed three dust trails emanating from the city, heading toward them. Hover-transports, probably carrying about five Martians each, approaching quickly.

"You better *hurry!*" he yelled.

The bundle was wrapped in a brown blanket and tied with twine. It was heavy, but she was able to carry it, lifting it onto her shoulder. Dropping it down between their feet, the two quickly unwrapped the package.

"A jet pack!" exclaimed Jett.

"And two auxiliary pistols attached to the back." Betty stuck one in her belt and handed the other to Jett.

"Quick, help me get this on," Jett motioned, as he slipped the first strap over his shoulder. "The Martians must have been waiting for them to poke their head up. They knew our ride should be waiting out here somewhere. We're going to have to shoot our way off this planet now and board the *Ares* in mid-air ... with this." He patted the jet pack as he buckled the last strap.

"Does everything always have to be this hard?" Betty forced a laugh, but her eyes showed concern.

"You could always take a desk job." He smiled.

Sand and rock exploded around them. The fast-approaching hover-transports were in range. The *Ares* whistled overhead again, this time with only one air speeder in tow.

"I think we're only going to get one shot at this, so we're going to have to make it count." Jett exhaled deeply.

"Have you ever flown one of these things before?" asked Betty.

"Nope, but I've seen a training video. Does that count?" Jett held Betty tightly against him and readied the control button for the jet pack. "Ready for lift-off." And the two were airborne.

The jet pack took a little getting used to. Well, actually, a lot of getting used to. Maneuverability was usually made with slight adjustment of body weight within the harness, but carrying an extra person made any real control extremely difficult. The unstable and wildly erratic flight pattern worked to the rangers' advantage, though, creating a more difficult target for the Martians to hit.

The *Ares* had doubled back, this time with the side door open again, ready for a retrieval. The hover-transports were fixated on the rangers, trying to prevent their escape, allowing the *Ares* to come in from behind, completely taking out one of the transports with a blast to its rear, sending the Martian occupants flying antenna over feet into the dirt.

A flurry of blasts was now directed at the rangers from below and above, as the air speeder fired at the rangers as well.

The two rangers returned fire.

Jett shifted his weight, trying to direct them in the general direction where the *Ares* would be momentarily. It was hard for them to get off a good shot. Betty fired several shots at the air speeder and one time nearly hit the *Ares* as Jett dove hard to the side, trying to dodge a shot that was too close for comfort. Jett was able to pilot them almost over the top of the *Ares*, giving the skipper enough leeway to roll the ship on its side, allowing the rangers to just turn off the jet pack and drop into the cabin.

A few blasts exploded the air next to the opening, pushing the rangers hard to the side, nearly causing them to miss the door completely. They had to react quickly and grab the edge of the opening with both hands and pull themselves in. But unfortunately, they had to let the laser pistols go.

The two lay prone on the floor, looking out the open door, watching the two pistols fall back to the planet below.

"Well, there goes another one," said Betty.

"Ow!" said Jett as the hot end of the jet pack touched his leg. He quickly unbuckled and scrambled out of the pack as the *Ares* pointed upward and went full thruster to break the planet's atmosphere.

Before the rangers could get settled into their seats, the skipper reluctantly asked, "Where's Eloi?"

Jett was grim-faced and paused for a moment, trying to think of how to break the news. "He didn't make it," was all he said.

He didn't feel like going into detail now, and there would be time enough later, he thought, to fully explain everything to the skipper.

The skipper tried to hide his concern. "Dat ol' coot." He shook his head. "I knew he'd find trouble."

Jett quickly strapped himself to his seat. "I need to send a priority transmission to Earth."

Betty immediately noticed a distinct smell in the cabin. The pungent residue left over from the Martian's two expulsions now mixed with something strangely familiar, a perfume-like smell, unsuccessfully attempting to mask the odor.

"What *is* that?" she asked.

"We scrubb da walls." The skipper gestured with his arm. "Not do much goot. Dat dirty skunk!"

"I thought this might help." Gus lifted up a large, empty glass cologne bottle. It was green and shaped like a rocket ship.

"He spray da whole ting too."

It didn't help much. In fact, Betty thought it only amplified the smell. Her eyes burned mildly, and her nose began to itch, starting at the back of her throat.

Within minutes they were miles above the planet's surface, when lights and warning bells came to life on Gus' instrument panel.

"We've got company again! Two Martian interceptors, coming in fast. Wait! Torpedoes! Two torpedoes! Brace for evasive action!"

"Stinkin' space rats!" The skipper flipped a few switches that released two pulsating decoys from the rear of the *Ares* and banked a hard right. One torpedo smashed into the decoy and exploded upon impact. The other stuck with the *Ares* and trailed tight.

The skipper pushed the thruster controls forward, increasing power, and banked a hard left. A blip flashed on his monitor. He checked it twice and said, "Dat'll do."

He piloted the *Ares* straight for a small round satellite that had four antennae, aimed at the planet's surface. At the last second, he nosed the *Ares* up, eluding the second torpedo, which collided with the satellite, destroying it.

The skipper straightened the *Ares* out and headed for deep space. "Where dey at, Gus?" the skipper yelled, while checking his scopes.

Gus' monitors gave no indication of the two interceptors' location. He even leaned over and looked out the windows. "No sign!"

"Don' like dis." The skipper checked his windows, and so did the two rangers in back.

Two blasts scorched the *Ares'* rear fin. "Above us!" barked Gus. "They're above us!"

The skipper yanked up on the controls and engaged the forward retro-rockets, full force. The two silvery disks zoomed past the *Ares*, having to dodge it on both sides to avoid collision.

"That was risky!" snapped Gus.

"Dat worked!" returned the skipper. "And mind your bidness! I'm da pilot!" He fired the forward blasters, hitting one of the Martian ships, sending it into a cascading series of explosions.

The other interceptor looped up, spun hard, and darted right. The *Ares* was a much faster ship, but the small interceptor had greater maneuverability and easily out-flew the old Earth ship.

"Nuts! I lost it again!" quipped Gus. "Who sees it?"

"Below!" cried Jett. "I thought I saw it go below us!"

The skipper nose-dived while barrel-rolling the *Ares*. He wasn't the most graceful pilot of his time, but one of the more daring. The two ships played this game of cat and mouse for what seemed like minutes, but in reality was just a few long seconds, until a smashing jolt brought everything instantly to a halt.

Jett opened his eyes. Everything was pitch black, except for the shining pinpricks of light from the stars outside the ship's portholes. He reached over and grabbed Betty's arm. "You alright?"

"Yeah, I think so." She put her hand to her head.

Jett called forward to the other two, "You guys O.K.?"

The skipper called back, "Yeah, but Gus, I tink is outa vit. He bonked his head, I tink."

The cabin of the *Ares* began to glow a soft red. The emergency auxiliary lights had come on. The artificial gravity was not working, and everything was starting to float.

Betty came forward and checked Gus over. The skipper was right; he was out cold. "I think he has a mild concussion." She leaned his seat back.

Jett went immediately to the windows. "Where's the other ship? We're sitting ducks!"

Betty went to the opposite side and quickly scanned their surroundings. "There!" She pointed.

Not too far away, the Martian ship was floating dead in space as well. Apparently, the collision had disabled both ships, and it would be a race to see who could get theirs repaired first. In zero gravity, Jett labored his way up to the skipper. "How do we get this bucket of bolts movin' again?"

"We took a bad bonk on da rear starboard." The skipper grimaced, shaking his head. "I fear da interocitor done got kaput. Someone gotta suit up and get out dare ta fix. Problem is, we only got one suit. It small, too to fit him." He pointed at Gus, who was still knocked out cold and hovering slightly above his chair.

Jett went to the cargo hold of the ship, grabbed the space suit, and brought it to the front cabin. Gus was only about five feet four inches. The skipper and Jett were well over six feet tall.

"Betty, stand up." He held the suit up next to her. "Looks like a good fit to me."

"I don't know how to repair a ship."

The skipper smiled at her. "Come. I show you how to put on," he said. "Dare is radio in hat. I'll tell you what to did. No troubles."

The suit was bright orange with bulbous rings at the elbows, waist, and knees. The helmet looked like a large upside-down fishbowl with a soft, internal head covering that bulged at the sides like puffy earmuffs. The skipper locked the helmet down, went to the front control panel of the ship, and flipped a switch, turning his communicator on.

A scratchy, tinny-sounding voice crackled in Betty's ears. "You hear dat?" asked the skipper.

"Loud and clear," she responded with a thumbs-up.

"Goot!"

The pure oxygen in the suit was a refreshing break from the mingling odors in the ship's cabin. Jett guided her to the cargo hold, helped her into the small airlock, and secured the door.

"You're breathing too fast," he said. "Try and slow down. Calm yourself. Belly breaths, through the nose."

He smiled at her and gave a thumbs-up through the small window.

She took a deep, slow breath, exhaled it quickly, gave a nervous smile, and replied back in same fashion. "I hope I can do this," she said quietly to herself.

"You do fine," came the voice of the skipper through her headset. She had forgotten that anything she said would be transmitted over the small internal radio of her suit.

"Well, here goes nothing." She opened the outer door and stepped out into deep space.

The boots had magnetic soles for walking up the side of the ship. Reaching the wrecked portion of the hull where the two ships had collided, she surveyed the damage. "Wow. We must have hit pretty hard."

The metal door that covered the engine was buckled badly

at the center and was flared out on all corners. She knelt down, and magnets inside the knees of the suit engaged to keep her from floating away. She grabbed the damaged door and attempted to open it, but it didn't budge. Repositioning her gloved hands, she tried from a different angle.

"It's no use," she said. "It's stuck badly. It's been smashed in pretty hard."

"Open da pocket on you right leg," said the skipper.

She pulled a large flap that was secured by magnets on the right leg of her suit. It revealed a varied array of tools that were held in place by magnetic strips.

"Got it?" asked the Skipper. "Use da pry-bar."

"Got it," she answered.

Betty tugged at a small crowbar, which snapped away from its magnetic grip, placed it under the crumpled engine door, and pulled. She felt it move a little, but it didn't open.

Glancing across the bow of the *Ares*, she saw the Martian interceptor slowly rotating end-over-end not too far from them. It was dark inside, and she wondered if the Martians were even still alive. Chances were that the Martians were in the same predicament as they were, and it was up to her to correct their problem first.

With renewed vigor, she pulled harder. The door still didn't come open. She wedged the crowbar into a tight slat where the door hadn't buckled much, stood up, and stomped it with her boot. The door snapped open, broke away from its hinge, and drifted slowly away from the ship.

"O.K. I'm in. What now?" she asked.

"What you see?" asked the skipper.

"I see two rows of silvery pipes that curve up from the engine and gather into a single chamber at the top that looks sort of like a metallic rib cage," she said. "There is a green triangular-looking thing that appears to be made out of glass. That triangular thing is smashed to pieces."

"Dat what I t'ought," said the skipper. "Da interocitor fuse is broke."

"That sounds bad," said Betty.

"You can fix. We bypass," said the skipper. "Pull flap open on next leg."

She pulled the magnetic flap on her left thigh. Instead of tools, this compartment contained miscellaneous pieces of small replacement parts that could be used for minor repairs.

"Pull da red wire from the fuse box," said the skipper.

She pulled the wire and looked up immediately. Something had caught her eye from the Martian ship.

"Oh!" she exclaimed.

"What?" inquired the skipper.

The lights had come on inside the Martian interceptor. That was a sure sign that they were making progress, and faster than she was.

"The Martians ... their lights are on already," she blurted.

Jett and the skipper went to their windows and peered out.

"We need to hurry," said Jett.

"Don't worry 'bout dat," the skipper said through the radio. "Just focus, and do what I tell. Now, take red wire from leg pouch. Da one wit' clamp. Clamp it on wire you pull out, den plug udder end in middle hole under triangle."

"Wait, wait!" said Betty. "What are you saying? Clamp it or pull it out?"

"Clamp it on red wire you pull out, den plug udder end in middle hole under triangle. Do now."

She grabbed the wires and did as he directed, at least as she thought he directed.

The outer lights of the interceptor came on and blinked in a rotating pattern around the outer edge of the saucer before it started moving. It stabilized, wheeled around, then advanced toward them.

"It's moving!" she yelled.

"Now get black wire wit' two clamps from leg. Get now!" implored the skipper, speaking very quickly.

"Got it!"

"Clamp onto black wire dat go to triangle. Den clamp udder clamp on piece of metal on motor, anywhere!"

The interceptor lined itself up with the *Ares*, apparently getting ready to fire.

She released the last clamp and immediately felt the vibration of the engine hum to life.

The *Ares* lurched from beneath her like a bullet. Laser blasts from the interceptor flew just below her feet where the *Ares* had been two seconds before.

The jolt sent her spinning. Small retro-rockets in the suit hissed automatically to stabilize her.

The *Ares* zipped off into the blackness. The interceptor immediately followed.

She watched the two specks quickly race off and disappear into the distance. Very soon, a sensation of loneliness washed over her as she considered her present circumstances, floating in the extreme silence and nothingness. The only sound was her breathing inside the helmet. She looked around at the magnificent acid-white brightness of the stars in deep space. They were both wondrously beautiful and frightfully horrifying at the same time. *What if they don't make it back?* She tried to banish the thought from her mind.

"Fellas ... don't forget about me," she said quietly into her microphone.

There was no response.

Just then, off to her right, shone a brilliant flash of light. An explosion. The deep space dog-fight was over. She couldn't help but worry now. Would they ever return to her? Would she be left here alone? She knew the suit only had enough oxygen to sustain her for about an hour or two, but strangely, the thought that pained her most was the idea that she might have seen Jett for the last time. That one idea pained her more than the idea of her body eternally floating alone in the vacuum of space and the short struggle she would have for breath when the oxygen ran out.

With each passing minute, her worst fear grew greater and greater. A tear ran down the side of her cheek. "Please be O.K. Please come back," she involuntarily vocalized the thought.

The red glow of Mars reflected in her helmet from behind.

Her earphones crackled. A familiar voice came through. "Can we give you a lift? It's not safe to be alone in this neighborhood at night." It was Jett.

She looked down at her feet. What a beautiful sight. The fuselage of the *Ares* was rising up to meet her from the dark space below. Tears flowed freely from both eyes now.

"Well, it sure took you guys long enough," she gushed. "Haven't you ever heard it's not nice to keep a girl waiting?" She took a deep breath and tried to conceal a sob of joy.

When Betty got back inside, Gus was just coming around, and Jett was trying the long-distance radio to reach Earth. Extracting herself from the space suit, Betty smiled at Gus. "Boy, did I sure miss you. The next time this suit has to be used, I would much prefer it was worn by its owner."

Gus returned a confused grin and rubbed his head.

Jett continued trying the radio. The small round monitor on the cabin wall showed nothing but static. The skipper informed Jett that the ship's antenna may have been damaged in the battle.

The ranger stayed with the radio a few minutes, trying different adjustments, until finally, a shaky picture buzzed onto screen of the

Ranger Corps logo.

"Director Freder, are you there?" Jett tried the microphone and waited.

Moments later, he repeated the action, then snowy lines wiggled across the image as the logo dissolved away.

The assistant director's face appeared on screen. "It's me, Jett, go ahead," said Handrix. "But be careful; this is an unsecured channel."

The communication was jittery and the signal very unstable. Jett feared that the damaged radio might give out at any instant. He thought for a moment about where to begin. Subconsciously, something didn't register quite right. He looked at the picture more closely. "You're not in the office."

"Yes, I've asked Maria to route this signal to my cruiser today. I had to attend a meeting in place of the director. Strangest thing. No one's been able to find him."

Jett stared at the screen, thinking for a few seconds, then finally said, "We've discovered who the ranger assassin is, and he's ..." Jett paused for a moment. "It's been killed. And ..."

"That's good to hear, Jett," interrupted Handrix. "How's Betty?"

"Also ... she's fine, sir, but there's more," continued Jett. "Frankie Malone's robot, there's more of those things. A lot more of them, I'm afraid."

"Go on," said the assistant director.

"Malone is dead, but he was tied in with the Martian syndicate and ..."

"Are you sure about this?" Handrix asked.

"Affirmative."

The screen fuzzed out with extreme static and gradually faded back in, but weaker than before. "I don't like the sound of this, Jett. You two be careful. There's been some strange ..."

Handrix once again faded almost completely away with heavy static, then briefly came back again. Jett thought he heard the words, "don't know where the director is ..." and "no contact ..."

There was one more thing that Jett wanted to relay to the assistant director, the most important thing, he thought. "Handrix, can you hear me?" he barked into the microphone. There was nothing but static now. He tried again anyway. "Handrix, if you can hear me, they've got something planned for Earth! Something big! And soon! Can you hear me? Soon! Maybe today!"

That was it. The radio was gone. Did his message go through? He didn't know for sure; chances were, probably not.

He moved to the front and put his hand on the skipper's shoulder. "How fast can you make this thing run, really?"

"She one of da fastest," said the skipper proudly.

"We need to make a bee-line back to Earth. I don't know for sure what, but something bad is about to happen—if it hasn't already."

CHAPTER TEN

ZERO HOUR

The early morning sky was cheerfully clear above the city of Metropolis. Parents would usually be waking their children and readying them for school. But today was a holiday, allowing most people the luxury of sleeping in before the parade and celebration to follow. Today was the annual holiday memorializing the deeds of nameless heroes from long-forgotten wars, and a celebration of the freedoms enjoyed due to the sacrifices of generations no longer remembered. All seemed like the beginning of an otherwise unremarkable day, until a blimp-shuttle captain nudged his copilot and pointed to the east. "Look at that!"

What appeared to be a brilliant meteorite flashed upon entry into the atmosphere and scratched a billowing, smoky scar across the sky, crashing in the direction of the old Grover's Mill Road. The crash produced an explosion that sounded like a distant sonic boom, reverberating the ground all the way to the outskirts of the city. Many of the curious and adventurous drove into the desert to get as close as they dared to catch a glimpse of the crash site. Some of the brightest scientists from Metropolis were immediately scrambled to investigate, and the local militia was dispatched to keep the crowds back.

A scientist in a silver, radioactive-resistant suit went down into the crater in an attempt to gather information about the fallen object, a bulky, beeping instrument in his hand. He slid partway down in the loose dirt, then stood at the bottom near the center mound. After running a few scans on his device, he turned and said to the group of scientists above, standing at the crater's edge, "Looks normal. Just your typical meteorite, except for its unusual size, of course."

The scientist made a few more adjustments on his equipment. "Hey, is there a communication tower nearby? I'm getting an exceptional amount of radio interference. Probably just an anomaly, though. The signal must be bouncing off the crater walls, since the direction seems to be coming from ... hang on"—he adjusted a knob, and slowly rotated his body—"the center of the crater."

A slight tremor was felt underfoot by all at the crash site, and the pile of earth at the crater's center began to rise. Dirt and rock shook loose, revealing a shiny, metallic sphere that eventually stood up on three slender, metallic legs. At full height, it was as large as a small-town water tower.

Those atop the crater stared in fearful awe at the spectacle. The scientist below tried to quickly scramble his way back to the rim.

With a few crunching steps, the metallic tripod was out of the hole and standing on level ground, its body slowly swiveling, scanning its surroundings. A single antenna-like shaft telescoped from its head, raising a pulsating beacon at its tip. The alien tripod towered menacingly above the crowd, as if ready to attack.

Civilians and scientists were evacuated, and the militia advanced cautiously toward it, weapons aimed and ready to fire. A piercing audible signal emanated from the machine that sounded like a foghorn on steroids.

The command was given to fire a few shoulder-held missiles, producing no result. Then the whole militia opened fire.

Another meteorite streaked across the sky, followed by another, and then even more. Eventually, the sky began to dim from the innumerable trails of smoke that blended into one ominous cloud, as the seemingly endless stream of meteorites descended like large raindrops of fire from the sky.

Within less than an hour, an army of these alien tripods began walking toward the city of Metropolis. The lead tripod extended its metallic tentacle forward. A bright yellow energy beam flashed and swept horizontally. Everything in its path, plant, animal, and human, melted and disintegrated in an instant. Only smoky, charred earth remained in the machine's path.

Zero hour had come.

Bright flashes of light over the horizon caused no small stir in town—most citizens of Metropolis had yet to find out what had really landed in their backyard. One of the militia men on the scene was able to send an urgent message over his radio back to base that sounded the warning, just before he was melted to nothing.

Like a swarm of hornets, the Airborne Sky Commandos were dispatched to engage the invaders in the fields east of Metropolis. Affectionately called the Rocket Men, their uniforms consisted mainly of leather jacket, knee-high boots, a single finned, brass-colored helmet and a laser cannon mounted atop a jet pack strapped to their back. The squadron was the first line of defense. Able to be airborne within a few seconds notice, the Rocket Men were fearless and almost as agile as a hummingbird on sugar. Their jet pack-mounted laser cannons were linked to a targeting system in their helmets and a firing button mounted near the thumb in their leather gloves.

The group flew high over the fields in several V formations to survey the enemy's position. They doubled back and scattered far apart before descending on the tripods. Several tripods swept their tentacles upward and flashed the bright yellow beams into the sky, causing the Rocket Men to take evasive action.

A few managed to dive between the beams and fire their cannons at the tripods' legs, tumbling three of the towering machines. But the tripod death-rays had incinerated almost ten Rocket Men from the sky in that very first strike. Descending from the direction of the sun, multiple squadrons of Martian interceptors swooped down to provide cover for the tripods.

The Rocket Men needed stronger back-up and a lot more of it.

Very quickly, the sky over Metropolis was streaked with silvery missile-shaped rockets racing toward the interceptors, where they soon converged in a titanic clash of subtle skill and brutal force. The XL5 Fireball Defender was a sleek, small rocket ship that carried a crew of two—a pilot and a wing man, both positioned prone at the head. The front half of this bulleted missile was made of a high strength plexi-clear, affording the crew a near 360-degree view of their surroundings. These Fireball Defender rockets were heavily armed with high-powered laser cannons and atom-scattering torpedoes.

Just before the interceptors were engaged, the sonic barrier was broken by some of the Defenders. Targets were acquired, missiles were launched, and cannons blasted with repetitive fire. Individual dog-fights broke out between the interceptors and Defender rockets as death-ray beams from below washed the sky with brilliant bands of crackling yellow. The sky became a canvas that grew increasingly darker, filled with black, exploding clouds and falling, burning debris of destroyed space ships from both sides. Some of these battles even stretched beyond the stratosphere, high above the city, creating a giant playing field of fatal tit for tat, each pilot pushing their machine to the limit.

Hover-tanks crested the hill in front of the city and faced off with the oncoming tripods. As the tanks fired their first volley in unison, a concussive shockwave rolled over the plain, and blueish concentric rings of condensed electricity pummeled the first line of tripods, causing several of them to buckle and smash face-first into the dirt.

The tripods returned their death-ray blasts and reduced many of the tanks to smoking, molten puddles. Although the hover-tanks were designed with a sloping mirrored front, intended to harmlessly deflect laser fire, the deflectors seemed useless against the tripod death-rays.

Circular patches of earth shook and twisted at the feet of a few of the tripods as a pointed, metallic screw swirled up from beneath the ground at each location. Telescoping metallic arms reached up from the subterranean machines and gripped the tripods by their legs, pulling them down into the holes as they retracted. Within seconds, metal crunched and tore into pieces as each giant screw spun, shredding the tripod to bits.

Badgers! The small underground attack squad had tunneled their way into position, seeking the pinpoint location of each enemy walker by seismic detection.

Hulking blue machines positioned themselves at the edge of the field, rolling on giant, linked caterpillar tracks. One of them stopped just off of the main road out of town and locked its brake. Small spigots extended from its four corners and sprayed water on the dry ground. Then, four large copper rods with sharpened tips were hydraulically forced downward, deep into the wet dirt. The machine was mostly a giant atomic generator that outlined the shape of its semi-circular, arched back. A small cabin on the side at the front held its operator. It had a large, girded tower at the front end that raised and lowered mechanically, with a giant, outward curving dish at its tip. In bold, electric-looking lettering on the giant machine's side read the word *Tessie*, named after the famous physicist and electrical engineer, Nikola Tesla.

A bright white light glowed just behind the arched vents, covering the Tessie's generator. The bright light quickly reached its peak and held at full strength for a moment, until finally releasing a violent lightning bolt that streaked upward to darkened clouds of smoke.

The Tessie quickly swiveled at its base, dragging the dancing string of high-powered electricity across the sky, and sliced two Martian interceptors in half. Across the field, many more of these highly charged bolts of artificial lightning were raised to the sky, and more tiny pieces of the silvery disks fell to the ground.

Over the hills behind the tripods came a wave of new Martian machinery—Spider Walkers. The Martian Spider Walker was a red metallic sphere with a clear, bubbled dome that walked on five legs. It was manned by two Martians and had twin rapid-fire laser cannons at its front and rear.

As the war escalated, infantrymen joined the battlefront to hold the Martians off from capturing the city, and the bipedal mechanical cavalry swung around and attempted to engage the enemy from their right flank.

In a secret location somewhere in Metropolis, a mysterious cloaked figure stood in front of a control panel. A wall of round video screens flickered as they monitored the progress of the battle just outside the city. The figure reached out, gripped a long black lever, and pulled it down.

Remote-control signals radiated out from a centrally located tower, taking control of all worker robots in town that had been purchased from the GISMO Robotics Manufacturing Company within the past year.

Throughout the city, worker robots stopped abruptly in the middle of their chores and walked out into the streets, leaving their tasks behind, many to their owner's consternation. Doors opened on their chest cavities, and high-powered laser cannons rotated down and locked into place.

The robots began firing on anything and anyone that got in their way as they headed in the direction of the battlefront at the edge of town. They would approach from the rear of the defending forces and, catching them off guard, would form a trap that would be virtually impossible to escape.

———

From the sky above the Space Ranger Headquarters building, a single, undetected Martian interceptor descended and touched down on the private landing pad of Director Freder.

CHAPTER ELEVEN

THINGS TO COME

The skipper, smart ex-military pilot that he was, approached the Earth from the dark side of the moon. Last night's moon would have been almost full, and he knew that the cleverest Martian invasion tactic would be to approach the planet under the moon's cover from the dark side while it showed its full glow to the planet below. If the Martians had chosen this route, it would be less likely that the *Ares* would be detected, trailing at their rear.

As they steadily approached, the skipper whispered to himself, "Oh, me, loogy dare." Then he jerked his head and shouted over his shoulder, "Hey, fellas, you might want look at dis! Bad stuff for true!"

Jett stepped up behind the skipper and looked out the front window. "Oh, boy, that's gonna be a problem."

Betty stood at Jett's side and put her hand to her mouth. "Oh, dear! The size of that thing."

There in low orbit, just barely concealed in the shadow of the moon, sat a Martian destroyer. It was most likely the flagship. The *Ares* was but a mosquito in comparison to this behemoth. It sat poised and ready to pounce, waiting for the battle below on Earth's surface to wage long enough so that the destroyer could swoop down uncontested and break the enemy's back with one final, devastating blow, sealing a Martian victory.

Gus stared stoically for a few moments and then said to the skipper, "How 'bout a mushroom seed?"

"Dat's whut I wud tinken." The skipper nodded.

Jett stared at the two thoughtfully for a moment then smiled. "You guys aren't talking about what I think you're talking about, are you?"

Betty stood ponderously, mumbling to herself for a moment, "A mushh ... you have a nuclear torpedo? Just how 'decommissioned' is this ship, anyway?"

"Can we get close enough to properly place it?" asked Jett.

"Dat's da trick," replied the skipper. "If dey see us first ..." He smacked his hands together as if squashing a bug.

"It's like this," said Gus. "We'll have to pretty much get our aim from out here. Coast in so they don't pick us up too soon on their scopes. Deploy the torpedo, then turn tail and run like mad."

"What's the odds of us pulling this off?" asked Jett.

"Dis pretty crazy," said the skipper.

"What other options do we have?" asked Jett.

"If they see us," responded Gus, "we're pretty much space junk."

"Then what are we waiting for?" said Jett cheerfully.

Betty jumped in. "Why can't we shoot from out here, then run?"

"That's what makes it so depressing," said Gus. "Their scopes would detect the signature of the torpedo's thrusters, and they would just simply fire on it, destroying it before impact. If we sneak closer by coasting up to them, nice and easy, like a small asteroid, we can fire the torpedo. Then when we turn and run, they will be distracted by realizing a ship was so close that the torpedo will have time to impact, hopefully doing its job."

"Hopefully?" replied Betty.

"Gotta aim it right," said the skipper. "Or ..." He did the bug-squishing hand gesture again.

Gus made all the proper calculations, and the skipper shut down the main power, keeping only the minor auxiliary cabin power on.

"Now"—the skipper stared straight ahead, fidgeting with his hands—"we wait."

It seemed like an hour as they gradually crept closer and closer to the destroyer.

"That thing is like a large mountain in the distance," said Betty. "It's so huge, it seems closer than it actually is. It feels like we're hardly moving at all. I sure hope this plan works. It seems like an awful long time for us to be exposing ourselves out here like this. Very vulnerable, to say the least."

"Ready, Gus?" The skipper put his hands on the control panel and prepared himself. "Gut ready for power oop."

At that instant, a spotlight flashed from the destroyer's mid-deck and swept across the *Ares*, then back and held stationary on them.

"Fire! Fire now!" shouted the skipper, madly flipping switches back on.

The torpedo spit forward, and the *Ares* immediately ducked right as the main thruster engines ignited.

"Full thrust!" shouted Gus.

Jett patted Betty's elbow and went toward the seats. "We better strap in!"

Three more spotlights came from the destroyer, along with an eruption of laser blasts. The blasts were so big that the concussion from even a near miss was enough to rattle the bolts of the *Ares'* sub-frame.

Jett looked out the side port just as an incredible flash highlighted the dark surface of the moon for an instant as the torpedo impacted the outer surface of the destroyer. Seconds later, sequential flashes began emanating from the interior of the large vessel.

"Look away and cover your eyes!" shouted Gus.

Two brilliant mushroom clouds sprouted simultaneously from the top and bottom of the destroyer. Seconds later, all aboard the *Ares* looked back to see what had become of their prey.

"Did we get it?" asked Betty.

"It's still there," said Jett.

"We not hit square 'nuff." The Skipper banged his fist on the control panel.

The destroyer had begun to roll to a small degree, and debris was everywhere, but the main hull was still intact. The most important thing for now was that the ship had stopped firing at them.

"Let's get out of here," said Gus.

"I'm wid dat!" returned the skipper.

Betty pointed. "Wait, look!"

The torpedo hadn't totally taken the destroyer out as they had planned, or even hoped, but the gravity of the moon was pulling the paralyzed hull of the wrecked ship toward its surface.

"Yea!" shouted Gus, making a fist in the air.

High fives were traded all around, even though they all knew that celebrating was premature at this point because of what still lay ahead. But they were all relieved by the narrow slip they had just given the Goliath.

Jett's face became grim once more. "We have to get down to Earth," he said. "Depending on how long that destroyer has been waiting here, I can only imagine what it's like down there."

"I'm on dat." The skipper adjusted course toward the familiar blue globe shining in the darkness.

Within a few minutes, they were descending through the high cirrus clouds above Metropolis. Scorched earth, the result of the fighting, was plain to behold, even from high altitude.

A red light blinked on the instrument panel in front of Gus. "We've got company again," he said. "Looks like our old green friends."

Five Martian interceptors quickly approached from below. Three broke off to the rear of the *Ares*, and the other two swooped up toward opposing sides.

The skipper handled the controls with great concentration, like a man possessed. "C'mon, you rotten toad-filth!" he shouted. "I grease my shoe wit' you!"

Just before the first interceptor fired upon the *Ares*, the skipper anticipated the action and evasively dipped to the right, barrel-rolling the *Ares*, like a graceful aerial side step. The interceptors overshot and regrouped, charging in unison from behind. Two went above, and the others came from below.

The skipper checked his instruments and barked at Gus, "Goot ready for shoot!"

"Ouch!" snorted Gus, snatching his hand back from the panel. "Bad static in here!"

"What?" the skipper gasped. "Shut oof! Shut evert'ing oof! All oof now!" He frantically began shutting all power off as fast as he could, even the main thrusters.

Gus gaped at him in disbelief. "Are you crazy, old man? What are you doing?"

The skipper simply yelled, "Tessie!"

Gus' eyes flashed panic, and he immediately ran his hand over the switches in front of him that were still lit up.

The *Ares* dropped like a rock.

The interceptors closed in and began firing. Two shots hit the tail of the *Ares*. One shot breached the hull and air began swirling inside the cabin. A flash of brilliant white clapped just outside the fuselage, followed by shrieking veins of electric current.

A Tessie had fired a lightning bolt toward the swarming interceptor disks that were chasing an old space ship across the sky. The shot fried three of the disks, and they fell toward Earth like spiraling pieces of burnt toast.

"Power on!" shouted Gus. "We still have two of them to deal with!"

The skipper moved the controls as the engines powered up again and brought the ship out of its nose dive. He noticed that the handling was now much rougher than before. A few of the retro-rockets that controlled subtle maneuvering were damaged.

"Stay wit' me, girl!" he blurted to his ship.

The two interceptors that had barely missed the Tessie shot recovered and attacked again, with lasers blazing rapidly. One blast came through the cabin, and sparks flew on the instrument panel in front of Gus. He frantically unbuckled himself and leaped to the rear, where the rangers were sitting.

"You not got away wit' dat!" snarled the skipper, gritting his teeth. He pulled a lever from under the control panel, which dumped reserve gear oil into the main thrusters in the rear. The *Ares* instantly began spewing a billowing column of ebony smoke from the tail. This was not a practice recommended for good engine maintenance—in fact, quite the contrary—but it created the necessary screen that the skipper intended.

The interceptors blindly followed the *Ares* down through the smoke screen, while the skipper turned the ship around on its tail, aiming the nose back up toward where they had been. He pushed the lever back in, stopping the smoke, and as soon as the two interceptors breached the cloud, he fired the forward cannons, taking both of them out.

Every warning bell was now blaring in protest from the front of the cabin. The *Ares* was shaking violently as the skipper wrestled to keep control. "Dis gonna be tough land! You betta brace!" he yelled.

Even though the lever to shut the oil from the engine had been closed, black smoke spewed out of the rear of the ship's main engine on its own, and now even from some of the smaller retro-rockets too.

The city was swiftly rising up to meet them. Betty saw a signal tower atop a skyscraper head straight for them as they began to yaw sideways. "Look out!" she screamed.

The *Ares* smashed into the tower, sending it plummeting to the street below. The ship careened into the side of a series of buildings, tearing a gash across the face of them, sending giant shards of glass into the air like confetti shrapnel behind it.

There wasn't much juice left in the engines now, but it was enough to roughly land the ship in the street. With a hard thud, the bulky ship smashed into the pavement, flattening the bottom and sending sparks everywhere. The nose of the *Ares* plowed into three hover-cars that were left abandoned in the street, tossing them out of its way like small toys.

The screeching stopped, and the ship came to rest in the middle of a deserted street, just a few blocks from Ranger Headquarters. Small streams of black smoke billowed from many cracks and holes in the ship's ragged carcass.

Explosions could be heard in the distance. The battle was making its way into the city.

"You guys going to be O.K.?" asked Jett.

The skipper reached under the front instrument panel and pulled out an old laser rifle. "I'm goin' huntin' for some more shoe polish," said the skipper. "Martian blood do wonders for leather. We'll be jus' fine, t'ank you."

Betty opened her mouth, lightly amused. She wasn't sure if the skipper was joking or not.

The skipper glanced at Jett and winked.

Jett stepped to the door, and the skipper asked where he was going.

"Rog said something back there on Mars that has been bothering me ever since," Jett replied. "I got a hunch that I'm going to check out, and if I'm right, I'm going to cut off the head of the monster controlling this thing."

"Where's that?" asked Gus.

Jett glanced grimly at Betty. "Ranger Headquarters."

————————

All of the major utilities for the city had been disrupted hours ago, but the ranger building had its own series of back-up generators, and the elevator was still working. This was a good thing because five hundred stories was a long way to climb. Jett and Betty reached the top floor and quietly entered the lobby. Maria the robotic receptionist was still at her desk. Jett put a finger to his lips before she made any noise to greet them. He walked over to the desk and quietly directed her to send H-13 to him immediately. In response, she pressed a button on a panel of the desk in front of her.

Jett and Betty could hear voices arguing in the director's office, but Jett didn't dare enter until first seeing the small Hoover robot. Shortly, the mechanical floor-polisher scooted on its rotating brush through an automatic door and quietly glided up to Jett. The ranger put his finger to his lips again, as he had done for Maria, so the small robot wouldn't give their presence away by his normal automated greeting.

Jett knelt down beside the robot and whispered, "Hoover, code words: Klaatu barada nikto."

A small panel slid open at the top of the robot's head, and Jett reached in and retrieved a shiny new laser pistol.

Betty smirked at the neat little trick.

"Alright, let's go," said Jett.

The door slid open, and the two rangers entered the director's office. The arguing was coming from the director's balcony, just beyond. Jett quickly made his way to the opening, and Betty followed just behind.

The assistant director was the first to address Jett. "Boy, am I glad to see you."

To Jett's astonishment, the director, assistant director, and Rupert Praxton were standing together with their hands up. A laser rifle was being held on them by, of all people, Eloi Lightfoot.

Jett raised his gun toward Eloi. "I don't know how you worked this out, but drop it, traitor. I'm not kidding."

"I know this looks bad, but if you'll give me a minute to explain ..." started Eloi.

"No explanations needed," retorted Jett. "This picture's coming into focus pretty clearly."

Eloi tried once more. "Just hear me out, Jett. I can explain."

Jett fired a shot between Eloi's knees that glanced off the deck behind him. "Drop it now!"

"O.K." Eloi calmly laid the gun on the floor and slowly straightened up. "Be careful what you do right now, Jett. You haven't got this all figured out yet."

"Quiet," said Jett. "Kick the gun over to Assistant Director Handrix."

"I wouldn't suggest that, Jett," said Eloi cautiously. "One of these men is an Oltercian. You know what that means? A manipulator. And whoever it is, I also think he's the man who killed your grandfather, the gangster kingpin, Xridåhn."

"Yeah, thanks for the confession," said Jett, very agitated. "Now kick the gun over. Now!"

Eloi reluctantly kicked the gun to the assistant director.

"And the way I've got this figured"—Jett addressed Handrix—"is that there has to be someone in the Ranger Corps orchestrating this whole thing. Someone in high position. An authority figure. Someone who could secretly operate above the law, while giving the appearance that he's clean. All the evidence points to one man, sir. The director."

Handrix was very obviously disturbed by this revelation. The director looked even more shocked than he.

"Unbelievable!" Praxton protested. "You'll be court-martialed for this! I'll see to it myself!"

"You can prove this, Jett?" asked Handrix. "You have evidence? This is not a charge to be taken lightly. You better be right."

"It's all circumstantial," said Jett, "but it's pretty tight."

Director Freder gazed at Jett with pleading eyes. "Jethro, what is the meaning of this? Don't be a fool."

"You know, Jett, I've had suspicions myself," said Handrix. "If you're right, this is a nice bit of work. Congratulations." He turned the rifle toward Jett, and his expression changed. "Now drop your weapon. I know you're a hotshot with a pistol, but don't dream of being a hero now. You haven't got a chance. Put it on the floor."

"Sir?" Jett couldn't believe what he was seeing.

"Do it!" demanded Handrix.

Jett knew he was right. It was a risk not worth taking. He dropped his pistol.

"Now kick it over," said Handrix.

"Handrix! That's it," said Betty. "It's an anagram of Xridåhn. He just manipulated the letters in his name like his face, or features ... however that works."

Xridåhn chuckled. His face contorted and changed shape. An unfamiliar dull-gray creature now stood before them. "You're pretty smart after all. I was actually surprised to see that you're still alive. You do realize that I paired you up with him to get in his way. Oh, I know I said it was the director's orders." He waved his hand nonchalantly. "It was really me."

Rupert Praxton's legs turned to jelly, and he fainted, collapsing to the floor.

Xridåhn looked at Jett. "She was supposed to have gotten you killed by now. I guess you're more resilient than I thought. But first things first. I like your original idea that the director is a traitor." He chuckled. "And you know what happens to traitors, don't you?"

"Unbelievable!" protested Freder. "You'll hang for this!"

Xridåhn turned the gun on the director and smacked his lips. "Believe you're wrong about this one, old boy. You're so gullible, I kinda hate to kill you. But you can't make an omelet without ... well, you know."

He fired.

Director Freder went to his knees and slumped over on the floor, dead.

"And now for you, clever boy. You've been a thorn in my side since the beginning. Consider yourself lucky, though. You've lived long enough to see the beginning of things to come. But that's all over now." He aimed the rifle at Jett and fired.

"No!" Betty lunged at Jett, pushing him out of the way.

In a single motion, Eloi reached for his boot and came up with his knife. It went deep into Xridåhn's heart, and he fell against the wall and slowly slid down.

"*What!*" gasped Xridåhn, struggling for breath. His eyes registered shock and horror, as if he realized too late that he should have killed Eloi first. "I should have ... I should ..." A few purple bubbles frothed his lips, and then he breathed his last.

Eloi went over to help Betty, who was lying on top of Jett.

"No, wait!" she said. She scooted over and lay on the floor, grasping her side. She was wounded. The laser blast had hit her instead.

"You alright?" Jett jumped up. "Here, let me help."

"No, don't touch it," she groaned. "It hurts."

"Lay still." Jett helped her straighten out. "I'll get a first aid kit."

A missile shrieked across the sky, just above the rangers, and exploded the wall of the adjacent building. The burst spewed pieces of office building and furniture into the air, and the concussion violently threw everyone to the floor, sliding and frantically grasping to keep from spilling over the side.

When the smoke began to clear, Jett rolled over onto his stomach and groaned. The explosion had taken his breath away. He sat up on his knees and looked around.

Debris was falling from the sky like January snow. The bodies of Director Freder and Xridåhn had been blown over the edge. Eloi and Praxton had been knocked unconscious against the wall.

Jett spun around. His pulse quickened. Where was Betty? He jumped to his feet. His thoughts reeled. Panic hit him in the gut like a twenty-pound sledge-hammer. "Betty ...!"

CHAPTER TWELVE

THE CIRCLING SKY

"Jett!" He heard Betty's faint voice from over the side of the building.

Jett rushed to the edge and peered over. A piece of steel trim had broken away from the building and was protruding at a downward angle. Betty was clenching an electrical cord that was slowly unraveling, connected to the broken trim. Sporadic wind gusts swung and twisted her as she dangled.

"Jett, hurry!" she said desperately.

His mind raced. "Hang on!" he yelled. He quickly surveyed the top of the building for anything he could use to reach her. Just to the right of him was a grouping of protective electrical tubing that ran the distance of the ledge. One of the metal pipes was bent and had a crack. He kicked at it, and it broke. He pulled and began bending it back and forth, trying to break a six-foot section free, thinking this would be long enough to reach her.

Betty called to him again, her voice dire. "Hurry!"

"Just a little longer. I'm almost there!" Jett furiously whipped the pipe to and fro, hoping for it to break. Precious moments were slipping, and the cord suspending Betty's life was about to give way.

Emotions welled up inside of him as he thought of all they had been through together. Handrix had assigned her to him to slow him down and keep him off his guard, making his own assassination much easier. What the gangster kingpin didn't count on was that she would end up saving his life instead—more than once. He couldn't stand the thought of losing her now. He had to save her.

The pipe finally broke free. He ran to Betty, sliding on his knees to the edge. "Here, grab hold!"

He leaned over with the pipe—just as the cord snapped.

Time seemed suspended for a split second as expressions of horror flashed across their faces. They screamed each other's names, and their eyes remained locked as her face fell away from his to the dreary clouds below.

His mind swam. His heart sank. His lips mouthed the word *No!* but no sound came from them. It was as if he was watching his own life fall away from him. Despair and helplessness sank in as he remained fixated on her silhouette, disappearing through the clouds.

Instinctively, his mind searched for a solution. "Think, Rogers. Think!" he barked to himself, but nothing came. He couldn't breathe. His stare remained riveted to where she had been just a moment before. He closed his eyes, clenched his fists, and yelled at the sky, as the last drop of hope painfully drained from his heart.

In that instant, he heard the hiss of a Rocket Man's jets landing on the rooftop across the street.

Jett sprang to his feet and started flailing his arms and jumping up and down, yelling to get the Rocket Man's attention.

"Rocket Man!" bellowed Captain Rogers, cupping his hands around his mouth.

The Rocket Man froze and stared questioningly at the ranger across the way. Jett had his attention. Once again his mind raced. He stood dumbfounded for a moment and thought of how he could quickly explain that Betty had fallen and he needed the Rocket Man's help. But he knew there was no time left. Precious moments were already gone. He frantically waved his arm in a directional motion and simply yelled, "Follow me!" and dove head-first over the edge, after her.

With toes pointed and hands firmly to his side, Jett stiffened his body as straight as an arrow to make himself as aerodynamic as possible. There wasn't much time to close the gap between himself and Betty. He wasn't sure if the Rocket Man understood what he needed him to do. He wasn't even sure if he would follow, but there was one thing that he did know for sure: he was now fully committed and determined that no matter what, he would not let Betty reach the ground alone.

With her back to the swiftly approaching pavement and her gaze firmly fixed on the circling sky above, Betty had finally stopped screaming and resigned herself to accept her fate. She closed her eyes and whispered a quick prayer. Then her thoughts immediately went to Jett. She regretted not letting him know her true feelings and wished that their only kiss could have been under better circumstances.

Her eyes began to water as she opened them. A dark spot on the sky was rapidly closing distance on her. She blinked quickly and refocused. Her heart leaped—it was Jett!

Spreading his arms and legs, Jett opened himself to catch air and slow his descent. With a dull thud, he crashed into Betty and latched on tight. "It's O.K. I've got you!"

"You've got me?" Her eyes went wide in disbelief. "Who's got *you*?" In that instant, she saw a vision of an angel descending from heaven through the clouds—with wings of fire. "Jett, look!"

"Yes, I know. Whatever you do, don't let go!"

"No, *look*!"

"Yes, I *know*. Betty, just promise me that you'll hold on like you've never held on before. Don't. Let. Go!"

Her mind was swimming, trying to comprehend all at once what was happening. Finally, it clicked, and she understood. She stared straight into his eyes. Her lip quivered; her voice cracked. "I *promise*!"

As the Rocket Man cleared the clouds, he saw the two rangers clutching each other and knew in that moment exactly what the ranger on the roof needed him to understand.

The rangers below were getting dangerously close to the ground. He engaged his afterburners. Two torch-like flames from his jet pack expanded in size ten-fold, thrusting him downward toward the rangers like a giant, double-barreled bottle rocket. The clouds above him lit up and reflected amber like an enormous cotton-ball filament. Like a hundred wailing banshees, the thrusters squalled and echoed back from the surrounding buildings.

With over two hundred yards still between him and the rangers, the Rocket Man judged that in less than three seconds, they would be nothing more than a gruesome stain on the pavement. There was no time for even the slightest mistake. Disengaging afterburners, he curved back in an arch, then, straightening parallel with the ground, swooped across the back of Captain Rogers, locked his arms under his shoulders, and clutched him tight against his chest. The weight of all three was almost too much for the jets to handle. The Rocket Man engaged his afterburners in short spurts to regain lift under the extra load.

Betty clutched at Jett with a death grip, determined not to let go—so much so that he almost couldn't breathe. She glanced out of the corner of her eye. They were now flying horizontally above the street, zigzagging erratically; it was difficult for the Rocket Man to control direction with the extra load. She let her leg relax for a moment, and her foot dragged the pavement. Reflexively, she immediately brought it back up and realized how close she had come to dying. She closed her eyes again and somehow managed to hug Jett even tighter.

The hissing rockets quieted as they began to slow. The Rocket Man instantly brought them vertical and extinguished thrusters.

With a short six-inch drop, they were all standing on their feet quietly in the middle of the deserted street.

The Rocket Man stepped away from the two rangers and raised his helmet visor. "Is there anythin' else I can do for ya?"

"No, that was quite enough," said Jett, smiling. "Thank you."

"Are you O.K., ma'am?" asked the Rocket Man.

"Yes," said Betty. "I think so. Thank you so much. I could never repay you enough."

The Rocket Man grinned big. "My pleasure." He gave a casual salute with two fingers and flicked his visor down.

Just as his rockets ignited, Betty yelled, "What's your name?"

He flicked his visor back up and smiled. "Cody. Chief Commando Cody!" In a burst of swirling dust and fire, he shot up to the sky and disappeared through the clouds from which they had just fallen.

Betty clutched at her side, groaned, and went to her knees, wincing. She was still in a lot of pain from the laser blast that had skimmed her ribs.

Jett went to his knees in front of her, putting his hands on her shoulders. "Are you O.K.?"

Through the pain, she managed a warm smile and thought of all the things she had wanted to tell him and started laughing. "Am I O.K.? What a silly question." She giggled, then forced a more sober expression. "Of course, I'm O.K. I've lost track of how many times I thought I was going to die in the last couple of days, but ..." She paused, the words backing up like a logjam in her throat. "As long as I'm with you, everything seems to ... What I mean is ... It's ... it's just that I ..."

He pulled her close, meaning to kiss her, but she put her hands on his chest and pushed back.

"No!" she cried.

Jett stared, bewildered. Why did she resist him? He didn't understand. Her eyes had a look of fear in them, and she began to tremble. Then the hair on the back of his neck stood on end, and goose bumps flooded over his skin as he heard what she saw—the familiar, shrill howl of the black creature from Mars. Putting all his weight on his good leg, he stood up, turned, and faced the direction of the sound.

There it was, standing on the ledge of a blown-out second-story window in a building just down and across the street.

The creature did an acrobatic flip. Spinning and turning, it landed squarely on both feet in the middle of the road, about fifty feet in front of him. The creature threw its arms back, spread its chest, and arched its back, letting out a terrifying squall of fury and pleasure, baring all of its frightfully sharp teeth. The pitch was so high and loud that a glass window pane behind them cracked.

There were two, Jett realized. This would explain the slight differences in the ones they had encountered on Mars. One had two small swords, the other had one long one. This was the one they had eluded on the train, possibly the brother of the one Betty had killed, and it was now seeking revenge.

The creature reached behind its back and removed its sword by the grip, clicking it into the fully extended position. It then started slowly stalking in a sideways curve toward Jett. He could hear the creature breathing from where he stood—raspy and aggressive, like a lion that had been severely agitated.

"Jett ..." Betty called to him.

He turned, and they exchanged a significant glance that took the place of a thousand words.

He quickly scanned the ground around him for something useful. Again, Captain Rogers found himself in a desperate situation without his gun to defend himself.

There, among the rubble of a smashed storefront, was a flagpole from the celebration preparations earlier, broken in three pieces. He reached over, grabbed the shortest piece, and put some distance between himself and Betty.

He figured that in a gunfight, he would most likely be the champion, but in swordplay, he knew this creature was ten times his master. After the creature went through him, Betty would be helpless—gone in a second. She had proven herself to be tough, but the pain she was already bearing was too strong for her to even stand up. He was willing to sacrifice himself for her once before; a second time made little difference.

He had no idea how well he would do, or even what he would do, but it would have to be over his dead body for this creature to get to her. Jett held the broken flagpole out in front of him with both hands and mumbled under his breath, "C'mon, you dirty boot-licker. Let's get this over with."

In a lightning-fast jerk, the creature flexed its wrist, sending its sword blade spinning so fast that it whirred like a giant fan slicing through the air. Like a gazelle, it leaped into the sky toward Jett, spinning and twisting its body so fast that Jett was unable to get a perfect bead on it before it landed right beside him.

Instinctively, Jett parried his primitive weapon and narrowly deflected the first blow. Instantly, the creature pivoted at its waist, bringing the spinning sword around to Jett's front. Jett desperately swung upward. A clank of metal upon metal echoed from the adjacent building as the two met squarely. The creature's sword had sunk half-way into the softer metal of Jett's pipe, causing it to stick for a second—this was Jett's chance.

He spun and gave a reverse thrust-kick toward the creature's abdomen, but the creature caught his leg squarely under its arm, locking it into place.

A toothy grin of satisfaction flashed across the creature's face as it stepped forward to gain leverage and violently jerked, snapping the bones in Jett's left leg like matchsticks, above and below the knee. The pain shot through Jett's body like a charge of electricity. The shock made him gasp for breath.

The creature ripped its sword away from Jett's pipe and immediately plunged it through the ranger's chest. Captain Rogers tried to cry out in agony, but managed only a slight whimper because of the hot, alien metal piercing his left lung. The black creature stood motionless for a rare moment, except for the horrible grin mangling its features.

Jett knew now that it was only moments before the creature would jerk the sword upward, slicing through the rest of his torso, and he would be gone. He decided that the last thing he wanted to see was Betty's face once more. He tried to turn to look behind him, but the pain was too intense.

The creature slowly licked its lips with its coarse black tongue and stared straight into Jett's eyes. It repositioned its hand on the sword for a better grip and began a low, gruesome laugh—then painfully hissed, releasing the sword and dropping Jett to the ground.

A pipe, dripping with the alien's own green blood, protruded through its stomach, with Betty pushing from the other side, from behind. She had used one of the remaining pieces of the broken flagpole.

"Alright, you awful demon!" she cried out, tears streaming freely. "Let's see how you like bein' skewered!"

The creature reached back and snatched her by the neck with its left hand, pressing its thumb hard into her throat.

Betty started gagging as the creature smiled once more, steadily increasing its grip, choking her. Within a few seconds, it would pull her close enough to snap her neck, killing her.

Jett gripped the sword, which was still stabbed through his

body, by its handle with both hands and began sliding it out. He could feel the metal grate like a grinding-stone as it slid against his rib cage. The pain was fiery, as if he was pulling his own soul through his chest by a string.

The cartilage in Betty's throat started popping. She kicked at the creature's knee, but it was much too strong for her.

Jett mouthed the words to himself, "One, two ..." gnashed his teeth together and, with a swift, outward thrust, withdrew the sword from himself. With every ounce of strength he had left in his body, Jett balanced his right leg under himself, stood up on his sprained ankle, and swung.

Three bodies simultaneously fell to the ground. Betty went to her knees, clutching at her throat. Jett collapsed flat on his back, and a jet-black alien body lay between them, sprawled forward on the pavement, separated by several feet from its head, pooling in its own green puddle.

Betty crawled over to where Jett was lying, and in a hoarse voice, excitedly said, "You did it!" She stared at him for a few fleeting moments and swallowed her heart.

The blood stain on his shirt was growing. She quickly cradled his head and pressed her hand to his chest, trying to stop the bleeding. "Jett! *Jett!*"

But he didn't answer. She could feel his unresponsive body growing colder in her arms. The blackness of panic grew inside her with every fleeting moment. She yelled down the street, "Help!

Somebody, please!" She received only the echo of her own words. Her eyes wet with tears, her voice faltered. "Ranger *down* ..."

She huddled close to him and pulled his body tight against hers. Her hands were trembling. She had never felt so helpless. She recalled his vehement protest of her being his partner in the beginning. Now, twice within one day, he was willing to sacrifice everything for her.

She pressed her cheek tight against his and said into his ear, "Jett ... you made me promise ..." Her voice cracked, mingling with hope and despair. "You made me promise not to let go. You made me promise, and I *kept* it—I didn't let go—just like you told me." An anguished sob tore from her throat. She swallowed hard and tried to fight back the tears. "Now I'm telling you, you stubborn ol' mule, don't let go. Hold on to me. Don't let ..."

Large teardrops lined her face. She embraced him tightly, slowly rocking back and forth on her knees, and began weeping bitterly.

CHAPTER THIRTEEN

PHANTOM AGENT

New, shining metallic banners had been carefully hung across Central Avenue for the late celebration of the annual Memorial Festival. Along the edge of the street, crowds began to gather for the parade that was soon to begin. Small, sprinkled flurries of confetti fell from the windows of higher buildings, thrown from the hands of children too impatient to wait for the official start. The sound of early morning celebration was growing with electric enthusiasm from downtown Metropolis, replacing the constant mechanical clatter of the past three weeks from the clean-up and rebuilding of the city. Condemned buildings that were beyond repair had been demolished and removed; many others were in varying stages of reconstruction.

The great majority of the population had insisted on following through with the celebration of the Memorial Festival, even though it would be three weeks later than its annual date. An energized feeling of patriotism and pride was renewed and invigorated, at least for a while, which had been apathetically taken for granted for so long.

A tornado-like roar tore through the air as a squadron of Rocket Men hissed through the city canyon, about five stories above the crowd, marking the beginning of the parade. A swelling chorus of cheers rose from the crowd below and spilled in through an open window on the eleventh floor of the hospital. Two Space Rangers were walking down the hall together, decked in their finest dress uniforms.

"Do you think he'll be up for this?" asked Betty.

"Well, if not, then you'll just have to be a little more persuasive than usual," said Eloi with a grin. "I really don't think he'd want to miss it."

Betty waved her hand over a sensor near the door of room 1124, and it opened. Grinning big and beaming, she said, "Hey, sleepy-head."

"Hey." Jett flashed a tired smile.

She walked over to his bed and laid a neatly pressed Space Ranger dress jacket on the nightstand. "How are you doing today?"

Jett grimaced. "Well, at least I think my ankle's finally better."

They both chuckled, but Jett stopped short, putting his hand to his bandaged chest. "Ooh. That smarts."

"Careful now; don't push it." She smiled.

Jett pressed the button to raise his bed slightly. "How are you getting along?"

Betty gingerly put her hand to her side. "The doctor gave me this awful, goopy stuff to apply to the wound. It doesn't hurt so bad anymore, but I'll be glad when it's finally healed, so I can stop wearing the stuff. I can't stand it. When it's first applied, it smells a little like a Martian after eating a coconut." She crinkled her nose.

Jett grabbed his chest again, suppressing a laugh.

"Sorry."

Eloi stepped over to the glass door by the balcony, then checked the clock on the wall. "We've got about eight minutes."

Betty held up the dress jacket. "Do you think you can put this on?"

"Why?" asked Jett suspiciously.

Betty glanced at Eloi, briefly, then back to Jett. "You know the parade is going to come right by your window. I thought we could watch it from your balcony. You don't want to sit out there in your gown, where everyone can see, do you?"

"What's wrong with the hospital gown?"

"Will you just do it for me?" she asked, smiling.

Jett glanced at Eloi for help.

Eloi put his hands up. "Not me. I'm not getting into this."

Jett reached out for the jacket, and Betty handed it to him.

"There's still something I want to know, Eloi." Jett sat up with some effort. "Back on Mars, we saw you change into Frankie Malone. And how exactly did you escape after all and make it back here? You've still got some explaining to do, as far as I'm concerned. Those details are still a little foggy to me."

Eloi was somewhat surprised. "You saw that, did you?"

"Yes, we did," said Betty.

"Well," said Eloi, "I guess I'll fill you in on my little secret."

A concentrated focus came over his face, then small muscles under his skin began to flex and move. His skin started to change in color, like a chameleon, and slowly became a dull gray, similar to that of Xridåhn. "I was captured soon after the doors locked down and we had gotten separated," he began. "They locked me in a cell, intending to keep me there until they had rounded up you guys. I think they may have planned on executing us all together—they really like their sting-adder pit and were disappointed that it didn't turn out as they expected the first time around. Shortly after, this Malone fella came to the cell to see who they had caught. I think he was disappointed to see me. Maybe he was hoping it was you?"

The noise outside the window rose and fell as the parade began moving up the street.

"I think he was getting ready to rough me up," Eloi continued. "He was holding an electric prod. Frankie had just removed his hat and coat when two Martians came running in. Said something like, 'we have them trapped in a service room.' Malone was so excited, he left his stuff behind. I saw that he seemed to have some sway over these Martians, so I got an idea. I grabbed his coat and hat and made myself look like this ..."

Eloi concentrated and slowly changed his appearance again. "This is the face that you saw on Mars."

Jett was surprised. "Why, that looks nothing at all like Malone.

But I could see how, from a distance, that I could be mistaken."

"Yes," said Eloi. "An Oltercian can't make himself look like *anyone*. I only have a few faces I can do. Some were more skilled than others and could do more faces, but I only have a couple, and I had hoped that it would be good enough to fool the Martians. After all, to them, most Earthlings look the same anyway. I tried my best to make my voice sound like Malone and started yelling, all mad and riled up. Some Martians came to check it out, and I told them that the old man they had captured knocked me on the head and switched places, locking *me* in the cell instead. They were reluctant to believe it at first, but when I said in graphic detail what I would do to them when I got out, they finally believed that I was Malone and let me free. Then I pretended to lead a search for Eloi, who, of course, is me." He smiled and changed back to the familiar face that they were accustomed to seeing.

"I had a similar idea to yours about what was going on," Eloi continued. "Stole a small ship and high-tailed it back to Earth."

Even though the two rangers already knew that he was an Oltercian, they were still shocked at his detailed revelation.

"How many Oltercians like you are there?" asked Jett.

"My race lives a little more than twice as long as yours does. I'm a hundred and forty-six years old. I thought I was the only one of my kind left. Naturally, that's why it took me so long to finally come to the realization that Xridåhn was an Oltercian like myself. As far as I know, I'm now the only one left."

A firm, hearty knock rapped at the door. It was the skipper and Gus, dressed as if they were going to a formal ball.

"Well! Goot ta see ya, Jett!" The skipper raised his hand to give Jett a good slap on the back, but when Jett grimaced in anticipation, he thought the wiser of it and shook his hand instead.

Gus was holding a vase of flowers. "These are for you, Jett."

Betty took the flowers and placed them on the counter.

Jett struggled uncomfortably for the right words. "Um, they really ... uhh, brighten the room. Thanks, Gus."

"Oh, don't mention it," replied Gus, smiling.

"Hey—" Betty turned to the skipper. "What happened after we left you guys at the ship? Did you see any trouble?"

The skipper laughed. "Ha! We *make* trouble."

"Yeah," said Gus enthusiastically. "You should have seen him. We started walking toward the battle and came upon all these robots walking in the same direction. Only they were shooting and blowing up everything. We were behind them, so Skips took his rifle and started picking them off, one by one, see? Starting with the one at the very back—so the ones in front wouldn't see and be tipped off—then worked forward from there."

"You done got some too!" bellowed the skipper. "And from long way shot." He held his arms up in front of him, as if he were sighting a gun. "You goot aim." He raised his eyebrows and nodded his head enthusiastically.

"By the time we reached the battlefront," continued Gus, "we had lost count of how many we destroyed. I'd say at least ..." He paused for a moment. "Well ... a lot! A couple of generals later told us that we probably saved their hides."

"Skipper, what about your ship?" asked Jett.

"Oh, dey fixin' me up," replied the skipper, eyes twinkling.

"Yeah," Gus chimed in. "The government was going to replace it, but Skips here asked if they would just rebuild his old one."

"Wit' a few upgrade too," said the skipper.

"You should see the new engine he has specced for it," said Gus, excitedly. "You thought it was fast before." He curled his tongue and whistled.

A chorus of trumpet fanfare blared from the street below.

Betty spun on her heel and gasped. "Put this on." She pointed at the jacket. "And get up!" she barked, as if it were an order.

Jett was so rattled by the command that he obeyed automatically. One leg was still in braces from the top of his hip down to his foot, so getting off the bed took a little effort. He gingerly stood, and Betty helped him put his dress jacket on.

"Please don't button it," he said. "It's too tight around the bandages."

"O.K. Let's go to the balcony now." She tugged, smiling a big, toothy grin at everyone in the room.

Betty held one of his arms and helped him hobble toward the auto-sliding glass door.

"What's with all this pomp today, anyway?" said Jett. "Look at all of you. You'd think the president was coming over for dinner."

They passed through the door and reached the edge of the balcony. The gathering crowd erupted in cheers from the street. An official-looking motorcade of flying cars was hovering just below the balcony.

"What's all this?" asked Jett.

The president himself ascended to the balcony on a small hover-platform and presented each of them with medals of honor for their efforts, which contributed to the squelching of the Martian uprising. He shook their hands and gave each of them a personal thank you, then posed for a stereo-photograph with all of them standing straight and proud in their best dress. Rupert Praxton was there too. He wasn't about to miss a photo opportunity with some real heroes. The president and the chairman stood on either side of Jett with his open jacket and hospital gown that went to his knees.

An aide handed the president a microphone, and he said a few words to the crowd. "No one is entitled to the blessings of freedom unless they are vigilant in its preservation." Scattered applause came from the crowd, then he continued. "Without the valiant efforts of you five heroes, the outcome of this struggle between planets likely would have been much different. An outcome we all shudder to imagine."

Jett glanced at Praxton. He was wearing his public smile for the cameras today.

The president continued speaking for several minutes before handing the microphone back to his aide. He turned and placed his hand on Jett's shoulder. "When you are healed up and able to get around, we'll have a proper ceremony in the park, where we'll unveil a monument with all your names on it."

"That sounds great, Mr. President," said Jett. "I look forward to it. Thank you."

"Thank you, my boy." The president shook Jett's hand once more and waved to the crowd, which erupted in loud cheers again.

After the president's entourage left and the parade continued, Jett asked Eloi what he was going to do now.

"Well—" Eloi stood proudly, almost at attention. "I've been asked to stay on with the rangers as an adviser." He tilted his head and pushed his lip out just a tad. "At least until they get all this mess straightened out that Xridåhn and his gang have caused. I think they're looking for a little old-school advice right now. Nothing official, of course. Kinda more like a 'phantom agent,' so to speak. One of my first bits of advice," he said to Jett, "is that you round up the rest of the main scoundrels involved in this insurrection, like Rog and his minions ... after you mend up, of course."

"That sounds good to me. But there's one thing I'll have to do first."

"What's that?" asked Eloi.

Jett put his arm around Betty and grinned. "Gonna have to run it past my partner."

ANDY HASTINGS is an avid time traveler, frequently blasting off to alternate futures as seen from the perspective of 1940s and 50s sci-fi movies. He lives on a ranch in South Texas with his wife and three kids where they raise moo-cows, cats and a dog. When Andy is not writing about futures that could have been, he is a graphic designer and collects antique toys, including vintage robots and ray guns.

andy@rockettreehouse.com

★ ★ ★ ★ ★

If you liked this story, leaving a review would be much appreciated.

www.ingramcontent.com/pod-product-compliance
Lightning Source LLC
Chambersburg PA
CBHW020024310726
48970CB00007B/2198